# Family Lost and Found

# Family Lost and Found

A Novel
by Drew Bridges

THANK YOU FOR
YOUR KIND INTEREST
Drew Bridges
10/9/2010

iUniverse, Inc.
New York Lincoln Shanghai

**Family Lost and Found**



iUniverse books may be ordered through booksellers or by contacting:

iUniverse
2021 Pine Lake Road, Suite 100
Lincoln, NE 68512
www.iuniverse.com
1-800-Authors (1-800-288-4677)

*None of the people in this book are real, and none of the events happened. Some of the places are real, but the references to well-known historical figures are simply context for a story.*

ISBN-13: 978-0-595-36955-3 (pbk)
ISBN-13: 978-0-595-81364-3 (ebk)
ISBN-10: 0-595-36955-3 (pbk)
ISBN-10: 0-595-81364-X (ebk)

Printed in the United States of America

This book is dedicated to all those who go in search of information about and understanding of their families.

# PROLOGUE: A FAMILY MYSTERY

## Colorado, 1873

(*Prologue narration adapted from the unfinished papers of Winnie Callum McBakery, originally intended as a work to be titled* Fathers and Sons: History of the McBakery Family.)

Sarah McBakery, sweating and tired from a morning of work in her garden, shielded her eyes as she looked up in the direction of the sun as it rose toward midday above the single line of buildings that everyone called "the town." The position of the blistering hot ball of fire at the top of the sky reminded her that her husband would soon be coming up out of the mine and would need his lunch. She put down her tools and went into the house, where she found her twin sons sitting cross-legged on the floor, giggling and pushing each other as they organized their most valuable possessions for the long trip to California.

Together the boys had selected a small square of cloth, placed it ceremoniously on the floor, and laid in its center a wooden toy gun, a length of rope, a few yellowish rocks they said to be gold, and other valuables that would protect and sustain them for the long trip ahead. They carefully folded the cloth and tied up the ends as Sarah gave them each a portion of cooked chicken, bread, and a few vegetables from the summer garden to take with them.

"All right now, get along on your way to California. But before you leave, be sure and go by the mine and say good-bye to your father. And don't eat all that food in a day. It's a long way to the ocean, and you'll need your strength."

The admonishment and meal were Sarah's usual contribution to the day's version of the fantasy that, if all went according to plan, would find the boys stopping at a big oak tree less than a mile out of town and wolfing down their food just in time to join their mother in the wagon for the ten-minute ride to the copper mine.

Each of the boys was rapidly approaching a size that would enable them to work together to keep the horse under harness long enough to plow one straight row. So far, however, each of their three tries had ended the same way, with first one of them and then the other spilling to the ground, resulting in the confused animal bolting out of control. Their father would end up on the ground with them, knocked off his feet by his own laughter at the mixture of success and failure. Each time, Sarah would come out of the house screaming at them, too late to stop what was going on, but forcefully reminding them of the damage to person and property that could result from that kind of foolishness.

The children were indeed large for their years, and only the absence of even the smallest bit of fuzz on their chins and upper lips betrayed their true age. They were not quite ten, but they looked much older.

During lunch at the copper mine each day, the boys recounted to their father what chores they had accomplished that morning. Sarah sat quietly and watched her husband eat and be entertained by the boys. On some days, Will McBakery came up out of the mine with the lifeless red dirt seemingly driven deep inside of him rather than just caked on his skin. Sarah and the twins could easily read the anger and despair in him on those days, so after eating the boys would spend those lunches playing in a nearby stream. Sarah would take up a position halfway between the boys and their father, watching out for the safety of the children while providing company to her husband and leaving him alone at the same time.

Few lunches were quite so grim, however, and most ended with all eating together, after which Will would kiss Sarah on the cheek, hoist the boys back into the wagon with a grunt of effort, and walk away, silently cursing his descent into the mine. Sometimes when he walked away, he would gather up the saliva in his mouth with a loud snarling and growling, and expel it with a sharp jerk of his head. The twins loved that and imitated their father as they drove away, covering each other with their spray of spittle and earning further scolding from their impatient mother. She needed a little less entertainment and a little more help, she would think to herself.

But on this day, when Sarah reached the tree, the children were nowhere to be found, and they did not answer her calls. Hurrying the horse along, she held her anger and fear in check, assuming that one of the other women going to the mine must have offered them a ride. She pulled the wagon to the usual stopping place as Will and a dozen other miners came stumbling out of the dark hole in the side of the hill. They filled the air with dusty clouds by beating their clothes and with the sound of hacking coughs and hungry, tired grunts and grumbling.

Will had seen nothing of the children, and when he heard that by then they had spent close to an hour in the noonday sun, he unhooked the traces from the singletree, mounted the horse, and rode furiously back toward town. He first rode toward the west and then backtracked east much farther than two small boys could walk. Finding no sign of them, he followed a dry riverbed that ran parallel to the main road, calling out to them until his voice grew hoarse. By mid-afternoon he was wandering in wide disorganized circles, and at length he decided that the horse did not deserve to die for the sins of his sons. He dismounted, walked the animal back to the wagon, and took Sarah home. His foreman yelled at him that the mine would not work itself. He told the man to go to hell.

That night, a neighbor came to the McBakery house with a story he had heard from a traveler about a group of ex-slaves on horseback who had come through the town late that morning looking for anyone who would give them work. The neighbor took pains to say that the person who had related the story was frightened because the men had been armed with rifles and some had been wearing old Union Army uniforms.

Will heard the story late that night when he came back from a walking search of another section of the riverbed, leading a dozen foot-tired neighbors, their lanterns dead. Will's face was fixed and angry. He traded his horse for a neighbor's fresh one, saddled, and left without a word to Sarah or anyone about when he would return or what she should do in his absence.

Sarah McBakery spent weeks doing little more than watching the horizon for her husband and children. With no horse, she was isolated and was only able to leave the farm through the kindness of neighbors. As summer passed to fall, she forced herself to spend less time in town questioning travelers and entreating those going West to look for her family. With great sadness, she turned her energies back to the practical side of living. By the first snow, she had the house sufficiently boarded up and food stores enough to survive the winter. She spent weeks alone, simply staring at the walls, the floors, and the wood burning in the fireplace. Neighbors called on her but could offer little. She asked for nothing.

The spring thaw found her desperate and emotionally paralyzed. She knew she could not plant and harvest a crop by herself, so she traded her land for goods to barter and bought passage back to Virginia with a caravan of busted settlers going East.

Sarah's diaries began only after she arrived in Virginia to live with her sister. The story of her new family and her children and grandchildren is well-documented in her writing and provides information for a significant part of the rest of this family's history.

Many stories were offered to explain the fate of her sons, Adam and Joseph. Animals, criminals, and American Indians were all frequently named as responsible parties, but as the story traveled down through the McBakery family, it was the story of the ex-slaves that drew the most attention, and this version was offered as fact by Winnie Callum McBakery, who married one of Sarah's grandchildren and was for a while the self-proclaimed family historian.

# CHAPTER 1

# AN ORDERLY LIFE

## A trip from Ohio to North Carolina in 1980

John Randt was the only child of capable and loving parents. He grew up in Ohio, living an orderly life. His parents ensured that he was never late for school, Little League baseball games, or piano lessons. His life, however, did not feel regimented or oppressive; it was orderly in a manner that, to him, seemed natural and nurturing. In fact, it was not until he went away to college that he realized that every family was not this way. He learned only then that not every family went to the trouble of writing the date on fresh raw eggs brought home from the store, so that each egg could be used in the order in which it was purchased. He was surprised that not every mother in America pinned socks together in the laundry so that no single sock would end up where lost socks go, along with the lost pocket combs and sets of car keys. Nothing was ever out of place, and nothing ever spoiled in the refrigerator in the Randt household. These were but a few examples of his orderly life.

This orderliness was part of what allowed him to be successful; he won the top academic prize in his high school, the valedictorian honor, and he applied and was admitted to an excellent private university. By the start of his second college year, however, he became aware that many students in his classes were in some ways more intelligent and accomplished than he was. He competed with them only by virtue of his remarkable organizational skills. No one worked harder or studied more than he, and he knew of no other students who wrote schedules of what subjects they would study at what hour of each day. These other students lived what he called rather "messy" lives.

He began to doubt that he would successfully compete for the best graduate programs in his field. For the first time in his life, he began to worry about his future. He discussed his fears with his parents, and as always, they listened without judging, offered examples, and shared experiences from their own lives for him to consider. These parent-to-child talks always focused on important values, and his father routinely reminded him of his options while his mother reminded him of their love. They were so helpful and understanding that, if the truth be told, they were becoming a burden to him. When he talked to other classmates who also found themselves no longer number one in their world, he discovered that, unlike them, he did not have an alcoholic parent, a broken home, or even a more valued sibling to blame for his problems. He reluctantly accepted that his shortcomings were his own.

On one visit home to his parents, he suggested that maybe he should focus more on his social life and asked if they would approve of his moving out of the dorm and into a house with some friends. To his surprise, they agreed. They seemed happy that despite a certain "stiffness" of character, as his best friends called it, he was obviously well-liked by many people. These friends were always trying to help him loosen up and relax. They teased him about his study habits and his lists. But they were genuinely excited when he told them that he would indeed join them in the small house a short drive from the campus. The first order of business was to throw a big party.

On the day of the party, John spent hours organizing his new home, his first home beyond his childhood home and the dorm. His housemates did not pitch in with the cleaning and fixing up, and one commented, "Give it up, John, when you see what kind of wreck this place will be next morning…that's when you'll need a mop."

Not grasping the real implications of such a warning, he contributed his part for the beer keg, literally the first one he had ever seen. Soon the party began. The house filled up with people he knew and others that were strangers to him. The evening actually began in a rather sedate manner until a certain young woman walked through the door.

"Category five, man, category five!" came a loud whisper between two of the partygoers as they pointed her out to John. He watched as this storm of a lovely woman, named Marie, became the focus of a newfound level of energy from the young men in the room. She breezed through the house taking control of the party, and soon began examining the contents of the refrigerator, where she discovered John's eggs with the date of purchase written on them. She found this hilarious and pointed it out loudly to all who were there. At this point John was a combination of just a little drunk and now embarrassed and angry. He asked her to please put the eggs down.

"Put them down? I certainly will not...but I will put them up," she said before laughing, and with an exaggerated sweep of her arm, she took one egg and threw it upward, smashing it on the ceiling above John's head. The yolk and white of the egg dripped down on John's face and shoulders. He stood there stunned for half a minute. The room became quiet. Even his more laid-back friends did not know what to do or say in that eternity of thirty seconds. Slowly, without expression, John took the remaining egg from Marie's other hand and broke it gently on her head, rubbing the gooey mess into her hair. They both burst out laughing. The party had now begun.

The party guests quickly brought the remaining contents of the refrigerator into action. Oranges and tomatoes became projectiles. Fencing opponents sparred with celery sticks. Milk and beer served as lubrication for the slide created in the long hallway, where people ended their rides headlong into a padding of pillows and bedclothes to stop their momentum. People opened cans of cooked peas, squash, and carrots, formed them into baseballs, and flung them against the wall, creating splatters of color declared to be "the new art." A delicious drunkenness engulfed everyone, including John, until the police knocked on the door and spoiled the moment.

John and his two roommates took a ride down to the police station, but no charges were actually filed. No laws were actually broken. The sermon by the officer on duty seemed to do the job. When John woke up the next day, he didn't quite understand why he felt so remarkably happy, with the gargantuan cleanup task ahead, not to mention the pounding headache from his first hangover.

Later that afternoon, there was another knock on the door. It was Marie, who came through his door again, into his heart and, that night, into his bed. It was his first real romance, and everything was new. They became constant companions. She pulled him into new and "crazy" shared experiences. They wrote and recited poetry in the streets. They went to movies and danced at the front of the theater while the previews were rolling. They got themselves tossed out of a restaurant for dancing on tabletops and for a less-than-successful attempt to start another food fight.

John felt as if he were holding on to a hurricane, now appreciating the "category five" description of her at the party. More than once, he told her that this kind of relationship was all so new for him, and she answered him one night that it was not new for her: "If you're afraid of the elements, just hang on to my wings; the storm will pass," she said as she fell asleep in his arms. He lay there and just looked at her for hours.

At the end of the summer, the storm did pass. She moved away, halfway around the world. And although they had supposedly reached an agreement that this would be the end of them as a couple, he couldn't just forget about her. He tried to call her a few weeks after she left. She was not happy to hear from him. He was devastated. He was confused.

John's confusion only grew when he went home for a visit and tried to talk with his parents about Marie. He expected that they would continue to be his perfect advisors. But when his mother realized that he was talking about "that kind" of relationship with this woman named Marie, she walked out of the room, more angry and upset than John had ever seen her. His father was only a little less reactive and seemed more concerned with the reaction of his wife than with John's questions.

Back at school, John tried to talk with his roommates and others about the reaction he'd received from his mother. He got no sympathy. Each of his friends went beyond John's stories to complain about their own miserable parents, blended families, mothers who went in and out of psychiatric hospitals, big brothers that beat them up, and so on. His grades fell and he lost interest in the academic achievement that he had worked so hard for all of his life.

He spent the longest time in his life without talking to his parents. He did not call. They did not call. He labeled them worthless to him at this point in his life and joined in with the rest of the students about how stupid and screwed-up parents were. He thought to himself, What is it with their damned buttoned-down lives and those plastic covers on the living room furniture unless there was company coming?

Other nights, he lay awake missing his mother and father. He didn't know what to do to make things better. He felt like an orphan, but he never said that out loud to anyone.

Out of this confusion, however, a new interest emerged. He grew more and more fascinated with the lives of his messy friends. He wanted to find a way to be as free and happy as he was when he was being dragged through life by Marie. He sought out troubled people and tried to understand how they were the same and how they were different from him. During a brief and rare visit back to his parent's home (not *his* home anymore, he said to himself), he announced that he had changed his major to psychology. His mother walked out of the room. His father did not reply to the information but did continue their conversations about sports and politics.

Through all of this, his parents did support him financially, and despite his new interests, he did regain his ability to make good grades. He ultimately earned admission to a master's degree program that offered a combined degree in public health and social work. In this program, he met Dr. Kingdon, a family therapist who offered classes and groups through which his students went in search of information and understanding about their family histories. This became John's passion, and he threw himself into this task methodically. Despite his present disdain for his mother and father, he wanted to understand more about what had happened in his family.

Dr. Kingdon held out the belief that every family had secrets, and he had specific strategies to guide the seeker to those secrets. There were particular things one should do and not do to find information. Dr. Kingdon encouraged John to do his best to declare a truce with his parents. When John described his parents as illogical, Dr. Kingdon answered that "everything is illogical until you understand it" and that if John knew enough about his family history, he would understand it.

John's new mentor advised him to go meet one of his relatives whom he had never met. He decided to visit his father's cousin's daughter, a young woman in medical school in North Carolina. They were about the same age, and he expected that they would have common educational experiences and that she might know something about why a certain set of cousins had nothing to do with the rest of the family. But Dr. Kingdon warned John not to ask that kind of question directly. "One finds those things out within relationships, not by cross examining someone," he taught. This made sense to John; none of the conversations he had previously had with his parents about this side of the family, or pretty much about anything to do with family, had been informative.

So today, he was flying to Chapel Hill, North Carolina, by way of the Raleigh-Durham Airport, a small regional airport still mostly in the countryside. The three cities nearby were steadily building one thing or another all around, but as John looked out the window over North Carolina, he saw mainly trees and open fields, interrupted by tiny towns and two lane roads. John took one last look at his genealogical chart, to make sure he remembered who was related to whom. The pilot cut back on the engine, the plane gave a quick shudder, and John came down out of the sky into a crisp spring day. The green of the season was much further along than back home, and the long slow descent gave him a spectacular view of the countryside. He saw small green buildings lined up along open fields and the man in the seat beside him explained that those were tobacco barns.

The passenger quipped, "Ahh, North Carolina, the state of the three T's…textiles, tobacco, and trailer parks." John laughed, out of politeness and at the cadence of the joke, but didn't really understand the humor. "Tha'd make a good country song," the man added.

The plane sat on the runway long enough for John to become anxious again about meeting his cousin. This was, after all, the "southern" side of the family. Somehow not getting the joke about North Carolina made it worse. He fidgeted with his notes and broke the lead of a pencil as he made a last note about a question he might want to ask. No need to be nervous, he told himself. He reviewed in his mind the phone conversations he had had with his cousin, Lee. Talking with her was comfortable; she seemed like an energetic, friendly person. She hadn't seemed interested in talking about family, at least not on the phone, but maybe in person there would be more opportunities, he reassured himself. She suggested the date for the visit, and it seemed almost too good to be true that there was a family reunion this spring. He wondered why his parents knew nothing about it, but it was an opportunity not to be missed. When he told Dr. Kingdon about it, the professor jumped up and down with enthusiasm, gleefully giving a name to the state of mind he wanted John to carry into this opportunity: a sense of "excitement and adventure."

Dr. Kingdon's questions had drawn John's attention to the fact that his cousin's name was the same as his middle name, and John wondered about a common ancestor. His parents knew of none, and when he asked Lee about her name, she seemed uninterested in the subject, returning in the conversation to the hospital in which she worked and which she wanted to show off to John. She did say that she had been to the reunion once before and that it was fun, mostly because of the food.

The flight arrived early, so when John walked out of the terminal to the obvious place to be picked up, he was unsurprised that his cousin was not there. She had said in her letter that she would wear a white blouse and had curly blond hair. He had mailed her a picture of himself. John watched several groups of people greet each other and sat down on a bench. Just then, a car pulled up to the curb and stopped suddenly. A blond woman with sunglasses and a white blouse waved at him. He did a double take, not sure this was right, because of what the car looked like. In his mind it was a race car, announcing its name, "Trans Am," in big yellow letters on the side over a black background, with red and yellow lightening bolts above and below the letters. A gaudy eagle was painted on the hood with its head poised over a raised air vent in the middle. The car looked like it had nostrils. Big mud flaps hung down behind the rear tires, two large antennae stood high on the back fenders, and decals advertising brands of oil and gasoline additives decorated the back side windows. He just stood there for a few seconds and stared at the car, until Lee yelled, "Let's go!"

She jumped out of the car to open the trunk for his bag. She motioned for him to get in, and they were out of the terminal area and headed out on the main road before they made eye contact, never actually saying hello. She was determined to get away quickly and kept her attention to the road. John looked around inside the car and saw that the inside of the car did not match the outside in extravagance. It was sparse by any measure, with no carpets on the floor and simple vinyl seats, except for the police radio that hung down under the factory-installed AM/FM radio.

"Like my car?" was the first thing she said to him.

"Uh, yeah, I do, uh…what year is it?" he replied.

"Nineteen seventy-six," she said, drawing out the words slowly as if announcing something wonderful. "It's my jewel. But it only has four thousand miles on it. I only drive it for special occasions. Plus, I lost my license for two years, and it just sat there."

"Lost your license?" he asked, as she pressed down on the accelerator, throwing him back in the seat. He reached for the seat belt and found a harness that fit like a life vest. It took a few minutes to figure out how to make it work.

She smiled at him and continued, "That's right. Got the car as a present from my dad for getting into medical school. 'Course I been fixing it up a little ever since. Kept pulling tickets around town, most of them nonsense, just pickin' on me. Then they caught me driving out of restriction. That's when they really came down on me. Really crunched me. Two years."

"Two years? How did you get around?"

"Not a real problem. I didn't go many places those middle two years in medical school. Dad was just twelve miles away. He took me anywhere I needed to go. Mostly I just studied. Losing my license was probably the best thing that ever happened to me. Made me get organized. I went for months without even getting into a car. Helped me finish medical school a semester early and get a jump on the internship."

John's mind raced with surprise, and he was not sure he believed some of the story, fast cars and speeding tickets being no part of his world. But he was also aware that he was looking at a gold mine of family stories. He made a mental note about wanting to know more about this father-daughter relationship. She had mentioned her dad four or five times without a word about her mother. But he came back to the moment when she accelerated to the next level of speed, and he realized that whatever the speed limit, they had to be going at least ten miles an hour over it. They were now out of city limits and in the open country. At length he was able reassure himself that she knew how to handle the car and they were not going to die. He settled back in his seat, checked the buckle on the harness, and watched the spring countryside fly by. Overhead, a steady breeze was pushing the clouds around and the temperature was in the seventies with no humidity. The windows were open, and the wind was fresh on their faces and in their hair. Slowly, he took his arm and reached it full out the window to feel the wind push it back with force. He smiled when it occurred to him that no one was going to tell him to get that arm back in the window or a truck would come by and tear it off.

They passed an apple orchard in full blossom, daffodils blooming between the apple trees forming a ring around most of them. Just beyond that display of pink and yellow was a freshly plowed field, the earth a deep, deep red. Crows and other birds were feasting on worms turned up by the plow. Lee interrupted John's reverie with nature: "You know, this car is the last really big one that Detroit will ever make."

"Huh…what," he muttered while coming out of his daydream.

"The car," she explained impatiently. "I said they will never make another one with this engine." She followed with a description of the capabilities of the car, listing horsepower, torque, and zero to sixty speed, none of which John really understood or could repeat back to her.

"I mean, sure you can get a Corvette or some fancy little foreign car, but if you're talking about pure high performance, this is the last of the breed. Gasoline will be four dollars a gallon and I heard this guy talking about how the oil will run out in a few years anyway, and somebody will invent an electric engine, and we'll all be driving around in little golf carts and going home and plugging them up in the living room."

Feeling totally out of the conversation, John struggled to find a question or comment that he could offer. He started to ask if the car had "mag wheels," but he realized that this was just something he had heard and he didn't actually know what "mag wheels" meant, so he stopped himself. Finally he asked, "So…I bet the gas really hurts your budget."

"I guess," she answered, "but like I said, I only run it enough to keep it in top condition. Can't let an engine like this sit too long. Couple of times a year I get out on these back roads and really burn the carbon out of the pipes. For everyday stuff, I take a bus around town. I can walk to the hospital in ten minutes."

With this she pressed the accelerator down, throwing them back in their seats. John found the armrest with his right hand but couldn't find a way to hold on that made him any more comfortable. It went through his mind that today was obviously one of those days to "burn the carbon out of the pipes."

# Chapter 2

# The Reunion

**Somewhere out in the countryside in North Carolina**

After a short drive, they noticed the scenery changing dramatically. In the middle of the rural landscape, the cousins came upon a gigantic road-construction project. It looked like a bridge overpass, with one level of road crisscrossing above another—two levels rising up above the two-lane road on which they were traveling. They looked both ways and could not see where this double-decker highway in the sky came from. Lee offered that maybe the farmer was holding out on selling the land, but the bridges were going ahead on the right-of-way already available. The contrast was striking—lush farmland as far as the eye could see, with a concrete and steel monster rising out of lifeless red clay.

"Got to be part of the Interstate Highway connector," she concluded.

They slowed to a crawl to ease over rough places in the short detour, passing huge concrete columns not yet connected to the rest of the structure. Bare earth was cut and shaped in mounds and curves, anticipating on-and off-ramps yet to be built. John and Lee counted a dozen yellow earth-moving machines lined up end to end, silent, waiting for action, after which they pulled back onto the intact part of the road, accelerating away from the construction and again into the open countryside.

They passed through a small town and were stopped by the single traffic light. John took this opportunity to ask his first question about family. Lee answered a few questions about her parents with a few basic facts and then turned the questioning around: why was he interested in these kinds of things?

"Just general curiosity," he said, not being entirely honest, "and because of this course in school. I told you, didn't I, that I was taking this family-study course?"

She nodded while pulling out a map and said, "Go on, I'm listening. Just keep your eyes open for road number 20202; that's the one we're looking for. God, am I hungry." She went on to describe taking calls at the hospital last night, sleeping only an hour or two, and then having no breakfast. And it was almost noon, when the reunion dinner was to begin.

"Well, see," John continued, "I have this one professor who teaches an intro to family dynamics course. He's brilliant. Everybody thinks so. One thing he said was you don't really understand yourself unless you understand your family."

"Sounds logical," Lee replied with a distracted tone as she pulled up to a small store, the only building within sight. "I'm starved. Let's at least get a drink and a snack." But the sign on the door said it was closed. Lee barked her disappointment and shot the car back out onto the road, scattering gravel behind them.

She took a deep breath, readjusted her position in the seat, and spoke. "I'm sorry. You were saying something about a teacher at school. Don't hold me responsible for anything I do when I'm hungry. Aren't you hungry?"

"Pretty much. I was just saying that I wanted to know more about my family. It should help me in my work. That's the theory, anyway." John wished he had more time to spend with his cousin. He found her charming under her rough edges but thought that he wasn't quite ready now to be walking into a larger group of relatives that he had never met.

"Well," she started with a big grin, "if learning about this family tells you anything about yourself, then you are a seriously weird guy."

With that, she laughed—she laughed longer, John thought, than the joke deserved. Even knowing this was friendly teasing, it made him uneasy. He wanted her to be more enthusiastic about his efforts. She continued with some real information about family, most of it secondhand, related by her mother—details about who married whom and who had kids, most of it information that John had already written down—but he let her go on rather than interrupt with questions. At least she was talking.

John was just about to ask a question when she shrieked, "We found it! The reunion!" As they came down a small hill, they saw a gathering of about a hundred people standing around picnic tables next to a church. Then they saw the sign on the church lawn: FORTY THIRD ANNUAL MCBAKERY REUNION. It was a reunion. But it was not their reunion.

Lee let out with a few choice curse words, describing how hungry she was and how lost they were, and pulled out the map. It didn't help. She tossed the map into the back seat and started to spin off down the road again, but then slammed on the brakes, sending John lurching forward.

"OK...we're going back," she said.

"Back where?" John didn't understand at first.

"Back there, where the food is! Your name is now John McBakery."

"Wha...that's..." he stammered, at a loss for full words.

"Trust me," she added, turning the car around and pulling into the parking lot on the other side of the church.

"You're not serious," he protested.

"I'm *starving* serious. There's at least half a dozen tables filled with food. They'll throw away half that stuff. Look: the preacher's praying. No one will notice anything except what they're stuffing in their mouths. We'll grab a bite and be out of here before anyone asks our names. Look at the license plates: New York, Florida, Boston, Washington, DC—and Canada! These people don't know each other. Do you see a California? I don't see a California. I don't see anything out West. We'll be the California side of the McBakery family."

Lee continued reading license plates and talking nonstop while John tried to understand what was happening. "There's some North Carolina plates, a couple of them, hmm...mostly East Coast. Nothing west of the Mississippi. Let's be from Seattle. Is that OK? Seattle?"

John was not OK. His fascination with people with disorder in their lives was still mostly vicarious. He turned his eyes away from the people who had concluded the prayer and were starting to fill their plates. He looked back at Lee, shifting in his seat to take her by the arm and tell her, "We just can't do this!" But he reached into an empty seat. Lee was out of the car and ten strides toward lunch.

He caught up to her and started to renew his protest, but she was paying no attention to his words or his state of mind. She stopped and gave him his instructions: "Here is the plan. We're from Seattle. You're my husband, but I'm the McBakery descendent. That way, we don't have to make up names. Use your own name; you won't get mixed up. Yes, that's good. This is our first reunion. We don't know anybody." She had him by the arm, a loving smile on her face, and together they approached the food.

Lee continued to whisper instructions and reassurance to him as they nodded hello to the first group of very friendly people. John noticed for the first time that Lee was quite pretty when she smiled, and people seemed to be responding to her as if they knew her, or should know her, and for the first time he began to believe that maybe she could pull this off. She handed him a plate. Without being critical or sarcastic, she told him that if he got in a jam, he should just point to her and say she was the one who knew people. He stood there a moment thinking that all of his planning for meeting family and for how this all would go and all his mental rehearsing were useless. Then it hit him how hungry he was, and began to fill his plate.

The tables were full for feasting. Fried chicken, ham, roast beef, sweet potatoes, sausage biscuits, and deviled eggs were first in front of them. The middle table had casserole dishes, yellow and zucchini squash, black-eyed and field peas, slaw, sliced tomatoes, green beans fixed five ways, and more. Numerous versions of potato salad were scattered about. Toward the far end were the desserts, chocolate cakes and coconut cakes and pies of all kinds filling an entire table.

Their plates were filled before anyone actually spoke more than a nodding hello, but there were smiles all around. An occasional smile betrayed curiosity, but everyone remained pleasant, and a few people actually feigned recognition. "Good to see you again; it's been a while, yeah…"—to which Lee responded, "Well, you know, medical school can keep you away from home more than you care to think about." The exchange seemed to satisfy everyone, and they went back to the meal.

Just before they made their way to the coconut cake, a thin man in a snappy pinstriped suit, who appeared to be in his seventies, said hello, identifying himself as one of the organizers of the reunion. His smile defined his question as one of genuine interest. "I'm afraid I haven't made your acquaintance, young lady," he directed to Lee. "I am Gregory McBakery."

Lee's response was smooth and immediate. "Then you must be the one who got my letter, didn't you? I'm Lee Randt and this is my husband, John."

Gregory McBakery did not respond to the question about the letter but continued to look her right in the eye, smiling, waiting for her to continue.

"Oh, maybe it didn't get to the right person. Well, I guess I should explain," she continued without hesitation. "We've never been to one of these reunions before, I didn't even know about them. I'm not sure *why* I never knew about them. Gosh, maybe I'm not invited, but…oh…this is a long story. See, this classmate of mine sent me the information. He…grew up near here and isn't a relative but knows about it…" All the while, she continued to help herself to the bounty of the table, tasting first one thing and then another and giving praise to the cooks.

"So let me see…what address did I send it to?" she continued. "I think I decided on Townsville. I knew that was near here, and with a small post office I figured that it would get to someone that knew about the reunion. I think I sent it to "McBakery Reunion Organizers" or something like that, you know, just having faith that it would get to someone...but it looks like I was wrong..."

She was starting to ramble, John thought, but he didn't think he would have known she was lying if he didn't know the truth. He felt strangely relaxed and more confident now that he realized this was going to work out somehow. A mouth full of deviled eggs brought some further degree of comfort.

The elderly gentleman kept the same smiling expression throughout Lee's story and responded with a reassuring welcome, "Well, it looks like you're in the middle of your meal, so I won't keep you. But as for your letter, I'm sure it ended up with my sister-in-law Mary. Her son works in the post office and that surely would have caught his eye. When you finish eating, you must meet her. I think sometimes that she not only married my brother but married all of us, the way she keeps us together."

Gregory McBakery repeated several times that he was not going to keep them from their food but then proceeded to tell them how delighted he was that they were there, to point out several key McBakery family members, and to describe how new branches of the family were found every year. Finally he squeezed both Lee and John on their arms and moved away with a spring in his step and a strong upright posture.

As the man left, John uttered a few whiny worries to Lee, who seemed unfazed by the encounter and whispered patronizingly to John, "Don't worry, we have a few more aces in our hand." She was now eating from the table about as much as she was putting on her plate. "See, I'm a doctor, and if anyone gets nosy about us, I'll drop that into the conversation, and they'll talk about their aches and pains and forget all about us." More potatoes joined the black-eyed peas as she continued, "But only because I'm a pediatrician. It's OK for women to be baby doctors...and people won't likely talk about their bowels. I swear if someone starts talking about their bowels, I'm outta here. And I'm taking my food with me."

Lee took a long look at the chocolate cake and decided she would have to come back for that. She and John turned away from the tables and looked for a place to sit. "This may be the hardest part," Lee mused. "I think if we go off by ourselves, people may think we need company and come over and talk to us." She bit into a chicken leg and kept talking. She spotted a group of people about her age, all with young children and announced, "That's the spot. They'll all be chasing their little angels around. If they say anything to us, we can just talk about how adorable the kid is. It'll work. The worst that can happen is I'll have to look in a kid's ear. This is a lot like a drug company lunch."

They settled into seats on a bench close to a young couple. The father had his two-year-old daughter bouncing on his knee as he ate. He was round like a pear and had a scruffy red beard and a nervous tic that made him blink his eyes fifteen or twenty times a minute. The child's mother wore a multicolored floral print dress and a floppy white bonnet. She sat in front of them, spooning small bites of applesauce into the child's mouth. To John the couple seemed too young to be parents, just babies themselves, he thought.

This time, Lee spoke first, addressing the mother, "Hi, I'm Lee, are you new at the reunion?"

"Sort of," she replied, shifting her weight to take the child from the father. "I've lived here all my life, but this is the first time I've actually made it here. I guess having a baby makes you want to do those kinds of things, and getting *him* here wasn't so easy either," gesturing toward her husband. He smiled, reached out his hand, and said, "I'm Billy, she's Phyllis…our girl here is Jenny."

"Well, this is our first one ever and we don't know a soul." Lee had assumed a new and different tone in this conversation, more shy and ladylike. John wondered if she had taken acting lessons or whether this was natural talent. "I'm Lee; this is John."

"Where ya' from?" Billy asked, squeezing his question from a mostly filled mouth.

"Seattle," Lee answered without hesitation, "and don't ask me how we got here. The only person we had even heard of on this side of the country was Mary McBakery. Do you know her?"

"She's my aunt, but more like my mother," beamed Phyllis.

John thought he saw Lee flinch a little, but the two of them struggled on through the conversation, some answers delayed by chewing extra long on certain mouthfuls of food, giving time to craft a believable answer that served best if it was a misdirection as well. Squeals from the children served as distractions to keep the dialogue comfortably disconnected.

"But truthfully," Lee recovered, "I haven't actually met Mary McBakery yet. Tell me about her."

"Well, since you're new here, when she gets here, she'll spot you immediately. Knows everybody and everything. I don't think she's here yet," Phyllis said, scanning the crowd for her aunt. "Aunt Mary is the one who knows all the good and all the dirt." John felt a twinge of excitement, thinking that this sort of family historian was exactly the kind of person he wanted to meet, but then did his internal double take when he reminded himself that this was not his family. The feeling turned to fear. Time to go, he thought. Their plates were empty. For the second time he turned to Lee to drag her away, and for the second time found an empty space. She was on her way back for chocolate cake.

After a few uncomfortable moments of silence, John was able to mumble out a question, "So how does someone, or how does someone like Mary, I mean, get to end up being a family historian?"

"Just nosy," snapped Billy, who immediately caught an elbow to the ribs from his wife, clearly not the first time she had done it.

"She is not!" scolded Phyllis, who proceeded to answer the question. "A lot of reasons. Her mother-in-law, Billy's grandmother actually, kept all the family pictures and records of the family, and when she died, there was no one else that was interested. And Mary was a Red Cross worker. She's retired now but just keeps on helping people, mainly here at the church, so people tell her things. She just finds things out."

"Boy, does she find things out!" came Billy's continued sarcasm, but this time he was quick enough to dodge the elbow.

Phyllis continued, "The county has a real health department now. I work there, but get Mary to tell you about when she was the only worker, the secretary, and the records keeper all in one. They worked out of this church. If you spend any time at all with Mary, she'll start telling stories…real interesting stories, like what people tell you when they're 'bout to die, or when they think they done something really bad and need forgiveness."

Despite himself, John's interest in Mary McBakery grew. He allowed himself a quick fantasy about how he could get to meet her. Lee was back with a selection of all the cakes, and John began whispering to Lee to fill her in on what he had learned as the various children broke up the conversation. Lee interrupted him with a question to Phyllis, "Who is the boy with the big glasses at the end of the table over there?"

"That's Dunnie McBakery."

"You mean Dummie McBakery," Billy chimed in.

"Shut your mouth and don't call him that. He's not dumb." Phyllis again corrected the behavior of her husband, with a tone that was leaving playful for angry.

"He is when he loses his glasses," Billy went on. "Every month or so, he breaks or loses his glasses, and he's totally blind." Billy was clearly building up for a story, but he backed down when his wife put her nose to his and just looked at him with no expression at all. It was a form of communication that Billy understood.

Lee interrupted with a serious tone, "I was just wondering about his eyes. I'm in training to be a pediatrician, so I was just wondering about his eyes." Here comes the doctor story, thought John, perhaps just long enough to get her through the cake, or to break up the fight between Billy and Phyllis.

"Other than the fact that he's blind without his glasses, I don't know what his problem is. He's a nice kid in a lot of ways, but he has a lot of trouble," added Phyllis.

"You really a pediatrician?" asked Billy, having picked up his daughter, mostly as a shield for his ribs from the elbows of Phyllis. "Hey, can you give Jenny her checkup, save us a bunch?"

"Sorry," Lee replied, "doctors don't treat family," and she looked at John and smiled. From that moment the conversation changed. No more questions about family, all about being a doctor. One question came after another—about how she got interested in medical school and where she was training, what she did in medical school, what it was like working on a cadaver. As best John could tell, it was mostly fabricated. Finally, the inevitable question came from Billy, "How much do you know about slipped discs?" This time, John got a wink along with the smile.

Before Lee could deflect that question, Billy's eye was caught by something else, "Oh my God! They let Granny Bede out for the day! And she's walking all by herself. How old is that woman, two hundred?" They turned and saw an elderly woman, thin, frail, with skin and hair pure white.

"And looky there, she's got Red Rhonda with her!" A young woman moved closely behind but not touching the older one, hand outstretched to give help if needed. Billy was back in narrative mood, addressing anyone around him who would listen, but directing it mostly to John, "She's a communist you know…Red Rhonda…went down to Chapel Hill on a scholarship but spent all her time marchin' and demonstratin' against the war. Now looks like she's back to takin' care of her li'l ole grandmother."

Phyllis looked weary but still had some strength to try to control Billy, "Don't call her that, she's…"

"She *is* a communist, goes down there to Hippie Hill University and plays with all those weirdo types. She's been in the paper for it. Embarrassed her poor old mother and everybody. She's one of those people that Jessie Helms was talking about when he said…you know…he said…he really said this, we don't need no zoo in Asheboro, all we gotta do is put a fence around Chapel Hill and we can just go look at what's inside of it."

John was drawn to the interaction between the two women who were approaching, to the attentiveness of the younger one. It was hard to think of her holding up a sign and yelling slogans. The older woman stood at a table and tasted something. A small amount of food oozed out of the corner of her mouth and dribbled down the side of her face. Red Rhonda wiped it away gently with her finger and looked around for a napkin. The old woman looked grouchy, probably in pain. Her wrinkled face made her look angry, maybe even dangerous. Red Rhonda kept the same pleasant, patient expression.

Several of the other men had gathered around Billy. They could see he was getting louder, and they seemed to be entertained by him. "Does everyone know about Granny Bede and the blue-gummed niggers?" At that point Phyllis snatched up her daughter and left, saying something to the effect that if he was going to go into that story again, she at least did not have to listen.

John was a little shocked to hear "that word," but his morbid curiosity got the better of him. "The what-gummed whats?"

"OK, here's the story. That woman is more than old-school...she's whoa-school. She's pre-school. Back in her day she got told that there were some black people had these dark blue gums 'round their teeth. The blue gums meant they were poison like a rattlesnake. One bite and you are dead, mister. No doctor can help you—that's just it."

One or two others were walking away from Billy, and he protested, "Wait a minute now—I ain't prejudiced myself. I'm just tellin' you what she used to tell us. And it wasn't just to make us behave or stay away from the railroad track; she really believed it. And all the stuff about the Jews...that too." Billy had a few people still around him who wanted to know about the Jews and Granny Bede. John was embarrassed that he was one of them, but he stayed.

"Let me tell you," he continued, "the thing about the Jews, according to Granny Bede, is that Jesus hasn't come yet...for them, I mean. So she grew up b'lieving that every time a new Jewish baby boy was born, everybody high-tailed it down to the hospital to see if it was the real Jesus." Some people groaned, walking away. His audience was pretty much gone. Billy kept talking long enough to again protest that this was not his belief, but that the old people used to talk that way. John stifled a laugh as an image flashed into his mind. He thought about carloads of Jewish people in a pell-mell scramble racing to the hospital, modern-day wise men carrying gifts of color TVs, U.S. savings bonds, and transistor radios.

Only the three of them—John, Lee, and Billy—were left sitting on the bench. Quietly, without the drama, Billy pointed out several more of the McBakery family members. The crowd was breaking up, with only a few lingering at the tables for seconds and thirds. A few latecomers arrived to say their first hellos. An elderly man, with skin so thin you could almost see the blood inside the vessels on the uncovered parts of his body, walked by awkwardly with a cane, almost running from his attendant. There was a look of delight in his eyes, not unlike the delight in the eyes of a toddler taking his early steps. Billy clapped his hands softly in applause for the old man's relearning of how to walk. He explained that the old gentleman's recovery from his deathbed was one of the big stories in town this year.

The three of them sat in silence, watching children in groups of two, three, and four swirl in play. On the shuffleboard a feud was brewing. The shuffleboard presently being used by some younger girls, several older boys tried to assert control under the pretense of showing the girls how to "really play." The girls were having none of it and one left to enlist the aid of her mother. At the back of the church, the young adults and teenagers had organized a volleyball game, with twenty people to a side and no obvious marked boundaries. A roughly-thirty-year-old man in a wheelchair loudly laid claim to his spot on the court, making it clear that he would handle anything that came his way. His overdeveloped, tattooed, deeply tanned arms stretched out to the side. He snapped strong fingers in a mock pinching action, portending assault to the backsides of anyone who intruded into his territory.

Billy spoke up, "Hey, let's get in the volleyball game!"

"Uh…I could use a bathroom first," John countered. He glanced at Lee, and finally, they were in agreement that it was time to leave. They sat for just a moment, surveying the shortest route to the car. Billy motioned to where the bathroom was located as he picked up his wife's abandoned plate and then walked away to the game.

Just then, Lee felt a tap on her shoulder and turned to hear, "Hello, I am Mary McBakery, and I am so glad you are here."

# CHAPTER 3

# OVER THE HILL AND INTO THE WOODS

**In a junkyard, beside a pond, near the railroad track**

Lee stood and faced Mary McBakery. John stood up but looked down at his shoes. He had been through several cycles of fear and then reassurance that they could pull this off, and now he was simply speechless, close to panic. He tried to take heart in knowing that having to pay for the food would be the worst thing that could happen. He knew he could do that. Lee realized that he probably was going to be so anxious that he was going to mess this up, and after some polite words of introduction, words that John did not actually hear, Lee looked him in the eye and suggested that he accept the offer of the boys at the end of the open field to play with them. John didn't even say "Huh?" He simply turned and walked away.

He walked directly toward the four or five boys who seemed to be about ten years old. They saw him coming and waited for him to get there, expecting him to have a purpose in approaching them. When he said nothing, one of the boys spoke, "Hey mister, can you skip rocks?"

"Can I what?" John had not quite made the transition away from Lee, but he was trying to relax and have faith that she could spin the yarn one more time. He would just stay out of the way. He turned his attention to the boys.

"You know, take a flat rock and throw it so it bounces on the water, on a pond."

"Sure, I've done that, plenty of times." He had not.

"Well, come on then," his new young friend said excitedly. "Got a game to win. There's this guy named Ben that thinks he's some unbeatable champ. We'll show him a thing or two." And with that they scrambled up the hill at the end of the field and into a wooded area. John looked back one more time and saw Lee and Mary McBakery still talking. Leaving them to go play in the woods with the kids didn't seem quite right, but several of the other boys were into the act now, yelling for him to follow.

He ran after them up the hill and found that just a few yards beyond the tree line was the railroad track. Two other boys were sitting on the ties between the rails, fixing pennies to the track so that the train would "squish out" the coins to three times their original size. He had never done this either. The boys explained that you had to tape them down. They were using some black electrical tape taken from home. Otherwise the vibration of the train would just spill most of them off the rail before it ran over them. Then there was the problem of finding them after the train passed. Most were scattered around in the gravel. You were lucky to find half of them. John really wanted to stay and watch this, but no one knew when the next train was coming, so he followed his newfound gang down the hill on the other side of the tracks. At the bottom of the hill, John found himself in a mostly overgrown and abandoned junk yard. Most of the cars were old and vegetation was starting to cover many of them.

The boys stopped, all looked at John, and gave each other quick looks back and forth. Then finally, one decided he would take the lead and speak. "We'll show you some blood for a dollar."

"Blood...for a dollar...I don't know..."

"It's Bennie McBakery's blood. It's in the truck that he and his grandfather got smushed in. It's right over there. But it'll cost you a dollar for us to show it to you."

John realized he had walked into a little scam, but he decided to play along.

He did know enough about what old blood and new blood would look like to ask them, "So how old is this blood? And who am I buying this from...what's your name?"

"Three years, I think," answered the boy who was the speaker for this deal. He gave his name as Stanley. "Maybe two years old. I'm not sure."

"Well, a dollar is a lot to pay for two-, maybe three-year-old blood. How do I know it's not paint or something else? Maybe it's just dirt. What color is it?"

"It's black, and...oh...I know it's blood, 'cause I saw it when it was red when they first dragged the truck down here. It was all over the truck. I know the story on the truck. A train hit it full-speed with two on board, Bennie and his grandfather. Never knew what hit them—pow! Never saw it coming because it was over there at the big turn. Got a gate there now. Didn't have one then, and they never saw it coming…" Stanley drew out the last few words for dramatic effect, and the other boys weighed in with how they knew all about it too; all said they could tell the story too.

One of them added, "It's a good thing Dunnie wasn't with them."

"You mean Dunnie McBakery? Bennie was his brother?"

"Yup, s'posed to be in the truck with them. He was home sick or he'd been dead too. His grandfather was thrown clear of it…want us to show you where he landed? He didn't have a bit of blood on him, but Bennie got all mashed up when the train rolled over him. It's his blood, but the grandfather didn't bleed…but he's still dead."

One by one, all the boys added bits of the story, trying to outdo the others with a little more grisly detail. John finally told them that maybe he would skip looking at the blood, but he did allow them to point out the truck and, for this, gave all four of them twenty-five cents.

"I can show you right where they picked up his grandfather," one of the boys said. "Everybody thought he was squished up in the cab with Bennie, but when they pried it open he wasn't in it. So they went walking around looking for him, and it was my daddy that actually found him. He was stuffed under a bush, just a scratch or two on him, so that's how we know that all that blood is Bennie's."

They moved on through the rest of the junkyard to get to the pond that was their original destination. Along the way, Stanley and his troop pointed out other famous wrecks. Stanley delighted in a grown man listening to him so carefully; this was not the usual for Stanley, so he gave John advice on other things as well. Stanley asked John if he knew why it was always a good idea to go to a movie when it first comes out. He explained that it's all about the popcorn. They bring in fresh popcorn for new movies. After a few weeks, the theater is not as full, and the popcorn might sit around for a while and might not be as good. This was only one of the things that Stanley was eager to tell John, to show that he was somebody that knew about things.

Upon reaching the pond, they had to partly slide and partly climb down a dirt embankment to reach a rocky sandbar beside the water. This was where they were to meet Ben for the rock-skipping contest. Tall trees, some weighted down with vines, bordered a small river with a wider and deeper part just in front of the sandbar. John could hear water rushing over rapids further downriver, and within sight upstream there was an old concrete dam, at least fifty feet high. In a shallow area between them and the dam stood out a dozen iron stakes from an old bridge, bent over from age and the force of the water, rusted partly away to the point that what used to be flat nail-like heads were now just misshapen lumps.

On the sandbar that measured twenty feet by ten feet at most were about a dozen boys. A skinny older kid with greasy hair stood on the bank above, holding a rope that dangled from a tree leaning out over the water. He kept threatening to swing out and drop fully clothed into the river, but Stanley taunted him and scoffed at his promises, saying "The water's too cold and you don't have the guts!" Several of the smaller boys had dug holes down into the sandbar, and the holes had filled up with water from below. With tin cans they had captured a few minnows for their artificial ponds. One had a crayfish.

"He'll eat 'em up," boasted the crayfish owner. The other replied, "Never. Never catch my fish…too quick, too quick, throw him in…no worry."

Several boys had removed their shoes, but no one braved the cold water for very long. The main attraction was the rock-skipping that the group had organized into a baseball game of sorts. One skip and you were out, two and you were on first base, and so on. No bounce at all was a double play, but if the rock made it to the other side, it was a home run, regardless of the number of bounces. Stanley told John that the current champ, who really was good at this, was "Honeybee" Ben. He got his nickname from a question in health class a few years ago. He asked the teacher how men could have more than one child if they were like honeybees, which could only use their "stinger" one time. Some of the other kids who knew better put him up to it, and the class howled with laughter for so long that the teacher had to send several boys out of the class.

Somehow, out of that legendary embarrassing moment, Ben and Stanley had developed a friendship, and although Ben would fight anyone else at the mention of the question, he let Stanley tease him about it. Ben was at the end of the sandbar, and Stanley questioned him, "Used your stinger yet, Ben?"

"Eat shit, Stanley," Ben answered in a monotone indicating that he expected the question and Stanley would be expecting the comeback he got. John watched Ben bounce a stone across the water for a home run. Ben's punishment in school for allegedly "telling a dirty joke" was short-lived in any event. When his parents were called in about the matter, they were infuriated that such things were taught in school. They thought health class was for learning about eating right and staying healthy. They tried to get the principal fired and kept the community stirred up for the better part of a month.

"Look out—here comes Buddy!" trumpeted a voice above the crowd. All eyes turned to the bank where a handsome blond boy of about twelve was jumping down the last few steps to the sandbar.

"Somebody better call the Bull!" the voice pleaded.

"Hey, Steve, I got something for you!" barked the new arrival.

"Does anyone know where the baby Bull is?" yelled the boy who seemed the one designated to announce that trouble was afoot.

"No really, I'm not shittin' you. I got somethin' for you, my friend." The boy named Buddy was taking large exaggerated steps across the sandbar and soon stood face-to-face with the boy that was obviously Steve. "I got it right here in my pocket." Steve stood silent, neither looking afraid nor responding in a way to provoke.

John started to ask Stanley who this "baby Bull" was whose name the one boy kept invoking, but he saw that Stanley had scampered up the embankment and was gone. Buddy and Steve stood in front of each other, puffing out their chests, and Buddy fumbled in his pocket looking for the thing he had for the other boy. Steve leaned back with a bored, condescending expression while Buddy searched one pocket and then another in an apparently futile search. What he finally pulled out, after his prolonged dramatics, was simply his own third finger poked skyward and into Steve's face.

Steve grabbed for the finger, missed, and came back with an open-handed slap to Buddy's face. They grappled with each other, Buddy pulled on his shirt with both hands, and Steve went down to his knees. As they wrestled, grunting and cursing each other, John heard a loud crash behind him and turned to see a dark-skinned boy who was almost as broad as he was tall come stumbling, practically rolling, through the underbrush just upstream of the sandbar.

"It's the baby Bull!" shouted a chorus of voices.

The boy they called the Bull hit the sandbar in full stride, put his head down, and smacked into the fighting pair, sending them reeling. "Get 'em Babe!" came the cry of the young crowd. The cheers grew louder and boys came out of the woods onto the sandbar from all directions. Steve lay on the ground on one side of the sandbar, and Buddy landed in ankle-deep water on his hands and knees, looking back at the Bull, who looked first at one of the boys and then at the other, asking them without words whether the fight was over or they wanted some more. Though he didn't say anything, Buddy apparently did not defer enough in body language, so the Bull pounced on him in the water in seconds. The Bull soon had the original instigator of the fight in a tight grip, holding one of his arms behind him and gripping his hair in the other hand, moving Buddy's head down to the water. He said nothing, but Buddy figured out what was coming.

"No! Stop. Bull, stop…I quit…It's over! Sto-o-op!"

By that time, Steve had disappeared up the hill. A remorseful Buddy sat red-faced in the water, head down, as the group of boys gathered around "the Babe," slapping him on the back. He stepped back from Buddy, flashed a big grin, took a deep breath, raised himself up to his full height, and just stood there basking in the praise of his peers.

Stanley, who had left and had summoned the Babe, had returned, and the boys drifted away back to what they were doing before the fight. John asked Stanley how this particular boy had assumed the role of policeman.

"Cause the Babe's all right," came the answer from a boy standing nearby who had heard the question. "The Babe don't want none of his boys to get hurt," explained another. Stanley just looked at John blankly, perhaps considering the question, perhaps never having thought about it before, and then looked away to join in the last few choruses of "Let's hear it for the Babe!"

John continued the rock skipping for long enough to hear from Stanley and a friend the finer points of skipping out of church. They explained that there was always at least one adult with an eye on the railroad tracks until the first hymn started, so you had to be either on the sandbar or at least hiding in the junkyard as soon as Sunday school let out. You could hide around the back of the church until the service moved closer to the sermon, but that was pretty risky. If your parents came to church, it was useless no matter what, but Stanley and his friend said neither of them ever had to worry about that.

By the time that conversation had run out, John's apprehension about what was happening with Lee had caught up with him, and despite the fact that Stanley was performing as a pretty good local historian and that John had runners on second and third and no one out, he said his good-byes and sprinted up the bank, ignoring the pleas of his new friends asking him to stay just a little longer. He retraced his steps through the junkyard and across the tracks and the open field and finally found the courage to round the corner of the church. Everyone was gone except a few die-hard volleyball players and people moving the tables back into the church. It occurred to John that the same scene was probably going on at the reunion that they should have attended.

Lee was nowhere in sight, so he walked to the car, and he noticed on the front seat what looked like cake wrapped in tinfoil. This encouraged him; it seemed unlikely that they were letting Lee get away with cake if they had found her out and put her in jail. He leaned up against the car and took time to admire the church and the well-kept grounds. The large church was old, but freshly painted. Its broad sculptured columns reached as high as three stories in the front, and it was a single piece of architecture, with no tacked-on brick additions to ruin the lines. Some windows were large clear panes, some of the panes showing obvious irregularities and reflecting the sunlight with a prism effect, scattering the light as John moved his visual point. The only stained glass was composed of faded blues and greens and was contained in two oval-shaped windows flanking the front double doors, and even those windows were more wood and metal than glass. A sign on the side indicated the church's age: "EST. 1854."

As he circled the front of the building, John took note of the cemetery that stretched out for at least an acre to the side parallel to the railroad tracks. Sitting on a bench was Lee, who jumped up and ran to him. "There you are! I looked all over for you. Are you OK?"

"I am now," he replied, his sense of relief both apparent and stated. "But…how did you get through that…that…meeting with her?"

She motioned for him to get in the car, saying she would explain as they drove.

They were quickly underway, and as he finished latching his seat belt, she reached out her open right hand to him. "Look, it's a gift. She gave me a necklace."

John took the necklace and couldn't believe what he was seeing. He didn't really know the value of jewelry, but this was clearly worth something. Up to now John had been passive and deferential to his cousin. Now he was angry. He stammered his surprise and protest: "You let her give you this…it's a valuable…it's…I can't believe this. This is taking things under…under, aah, false pretenses or something."

Lee kept driving without looking at him or betraying any emotion. He stared at her and then demanded that she speak and explain this. She took one quick glance at him and said, "I guess that's one way to think about it."

Stunned by her actions and her attitude, John wondered to himself what exactly he was dealing with in this cousin that he had known for maybe two hours. The word "psychopath" and a few others he had learned at school came into his mind. At a loss for something else to say, he sat wordlessly, sighing and grunting. Her anger grew as well, and they moved on down the road practically hissing at each other.

Just then, a police car appeared behind them, lights flashing. Lee slowed and moved to the right, thinking that the officer needed to get around, but he pulled in behind them and gave his siren a short blast. He motioned for them to pull over. John's mind flooded with panic: "Oh my God! Oh my God! You've done it now! He'll arrest us!"

Lee told him to shut up, that this was probably another one of those routine stops she got all the time, some young guy policeman wanting to have a look at the car or the blond girl. She said she would handle it if John would just keep his mouth closed.

The officer got out of the cruiser, steadied his hat on his head as he approached the driver's side door, and spoke, "Excuse me ma'am, are you the young lady that just left after visiting with Mrs. McBakery?"

# CHAPTER 4

# AN ACT OF KINDNESS

**In a trailer park near Warrenton, North Carolina**

John saw a sign of vulnerability in his cousin for the first time when the officer, handsome and square-jawed with a crisp, clean uniform and a large pistol and nightstick on his belt, poked his head through the window. Lee looked up at him, all of the rose gone from her cheeks, looking very much like a little girl waiting to be reprimanded. Through his fog of fear, it took John a few minutes to realize that was not what was happening.

"Ma'am," started the officer with utmost politeness, "my aunt, Mary McBakery called me and told me she had just missed you when you drove away, and...uh...she described your car and asked me if I could catch you. See, I'm a deputy here in town, name's Miles, and well, my aunt...one named Mary...said they got a boy that's been hurt over at the church. And Mary told me you were a doctor." Lee let go of her grip on the steering wheel. It took John a little longer to exhale.

The deputy continued, "See, this is the thing: the hospital in Warrenton closed a few years ago, and we could take him down to Hen'erson, or down to Duke, but either place, we'd be sittin' for four, five hours. And he don't seem real bad-off hurt, so maybe, you could just take a quick look at him and tell us whether he needs to go to a hospital. My aunt said to ask you if you would do it and that it would be a real act of kindness to our family if you would do it."

All Lee said was that she would and the officer returned to his car and pulled back on the road to lead the way to the injured boy. By the time they returned to the church, Mary McBakery had taken the child back to his home to make sure his mother knew this was going on. When the deputy came back to tell them they needed to go somewhere else, he paused to look at Lee's car. He lingered just a minute, admiring it, and asked, "This thing run…or is it just for show?"

"It'll run a little," Lee answered with a nonchalance that came from having been asked the question often.

Officer Miles returned to the patrol car and seemed to offer a challenge by the way he sped off, tires squealing on the pavement. Lee moved out on the road, stopped, flashed a wide grin at John, and then pressed the accelerator flat to the floor. The back tires billowed black smoke, giving out a high-pitched screech as they spun on the pavement, the car not yet moving forward, but seeming to slide sideways a few feet. Lee let off the accelerator and the tires caught traction, rocketing the car down the road. The police cruiser's twenty-second lead evaporated in seconds as they pulled right up on the deputy's rear bumper. They watched him take off his hat and wave it like he was fanning himself from the heat, and Lee laughed. She and the deputy had some communication going on that John didn't quite understand, partly due to the fact that he was trying hard to not throw up.

Both drivers slowed and obeyed the speed limit for the rest of the short ride. Their destination turned out to be the PineCrest Mobile Home Park #4. John remembered the joke about "textiles, tobacco, and trailer parks" and felt some satisfaction at finding out what the man on the airplane was talking about. He saw nothing that resembled a crest of a hill and no pine trees, truthfully no trees at all in either direction among the at-least fifty rectangular mobile-home units that were packed closely together and that all looked pretty much the same, yards filled with both children's toys, most of them broken, and automobiles, most of them broken down with weeds growing up around the tires and bumpers. All the mobile homes that were nearby had window air conditioners running full blast to fight the sun that was unimpeded by any shade.

As the officer left his car, he laughed and said, "Lady, if you doctor the way you drive, then Dunnie McBakery is going to be just fine."

"Dunnie McBakery? The kid with the big glasses? That's who we're going to see? The same one that was at the reunion?" Lee questioned the officer.

"There ain't but one Dunnie McBakery," answered the officer.

They entered the trailer by steps made of cinder blocks and had to use some degree of balance to negotiate a door that didn't quite fit on the hinges. Dunnie McBakery lay on the couch in the main living area, his eyes closed and his body covered to the waist by a blanket. His broken glasses, lying on a table beside the couch, caught both Lee and John's eyes. Small flecks of blood remained on the one unbroken lens. Even at Lee and John's first glance, Dunnie's face announced that it was the source of the blood. The several small cuts around his eyes and nose no longer bled freely, but the dried encrustations were surrounded by red and black bruises just emerging around both of his eyes.

Dunnie heard the group enter the room and raised himself up to look at them through squinting eyes. Lee came out from behind Officer Miles and went directly to the child and introduced herself, "Hi there, you must be Dunnie; my name is Dr. Randt," and stuck out her hand in greeting. "Looks like you've had a little trouble."

"Mama!" the boy cried. A woman about forty years old, Dunnie's mother, Betty, stepped through a doorway from a back room. Lee smiled at Dunnie and stepped back toward his mother, extending her hand and introducing herself again. The woman offered a floppy hand for Lee to grasp, but did not really shake hands or make eye contact. She seated herself in a chair near an open window, pulling a worn bathrobe more tightly around her.

The deputy spoke up to make it clear who everyone was and to tell how Mary McBakery had come upon Dunnie walking down the road by the church, holding his glasses in his hand and crying, and how it was Mary's idea that he should be examined in this way. Neither seeking consent nor receiving it, Miles motioned that it was OK for Lee to proceed. Lee asked the mother directly if she had permission to examine Dunnie. Betty McBakery nodded and mumbled, "OK." Lee nodded toward the deputy, who shuffled his feet nervously, making audible scratching sounds on the floor.

Lee again approached the boy who renewed his protest with more of a whimper than a real challenge. "For God's sake, let her look!" snapped the mother from across the room. Lee kneeled down in front of Dunnie to look at him directly. She offered a smile, and this time he returned it.

"Looks like you got some pretty bad scratches there. Do they hurt?"

"No," he mumbled, looking away.

"Did you get hurt anywhere else?"

"No," came the tight-lipped reply.

"Can you sit up? Are you dizzy?" Lee continued. With that question Dunnie threw off the blanket and stood up all in one motion.

"Whoa, there, my little man, let's not go too fast. Sit back down and let me look."

"I fell down," said Dunnie softly.

"His father hit him!" boomed his mother from across the room.

"No. I fell down," Dunnie insisted, louder the second time.

"That doesn't matter right now," put in Lee. "All that matters is that we make sure you're OK. Does anyone have a flashlight?" Dunnie whined again, even with Lee's reassurance that all she was going to do was look at his eyes.

"I told you to let the lady look!" puffed his mother from across the room, lighting up a cigarette. Dunnie began to cry softly but said it was all right for her to look in his eyes with the flashlight from the deputy's belt. In just a few minutes, the tone in the room changed entirely, as the young patient went through Lee's exam. She checked his eyes to see if the pupils dilated symmetrically and then handed the flashlight to Dunnie to have him check hers. That was enough to calm and charm him, and ultimately he was giggling playfully as she asked him to do some things that seemed like games but were a version of her diagnostic tests. They took turns walking a straight line, hopping on one foot, opening and closing eyes, and making eyebrows go up and down. A little game of peek-a-boo was explained as a test of vision and coordination. Lacking a stethoscope, Lee used her hands to make sure both sides of his chest inflated equally, thumped on his back with the ends of her fingers, and pronounced him "good to go." She determined that he was hungry enough to eat something, and after his mother made him a sandwich, she had him go into the bedroom to lie down "while the grownups talk."

"So…next step?" began Lee, looking first at the officer and then at the mother.

"Next step?" simultaneously from both of them.

"Next step meaning some sort of legal action…about the crime that has just been committed here." Lee spoke slowly in a somewhat preachy tone.

"Oh, that'd be great, wouldn't it? His mother out of work and his daddy in jail. That'd be real good for the boy," answered his mother. The deputy added that this thing happened from time to time and that he would talk to Jake McBakery to make sure that he would not be so rough with Dunnie. Lee did not seem surprised at the answers and the attitudes. John thought to himself that it looked like she had been through this before.

"There's this little matter of child abuse laws," returned Lee, directing her reply mostly to the officer. "As a law enforcement officer, I believe that you would be familiar with those."

Before the deputy could reply, Dunnie's mother was on her feet and up in Lee's face. "Look lady, I don't know who you are or who the hell you think you are, but this is not your business. You don't know shit about what goes on here. That boy knows very well the same thing that I know—that when his daddy's a certain way, you stay back. But sometimes Dunnie don't listen, so Dunnie's got to learn. He was whinin' and pullin' on his father all the livelong day, on the only day in a long time that he had time to get some rest. I told him to leave his daddy alone, but he wouldn't listen. He just kep' on, and on, so Jake gave him a little smack. If he'd just not hit him in the face, no one would have known a thing about it."

The mother's face was flushed and there were tears in her eyes. She continued. "His daddy has a point when he's goin' to lose all his senses, and if you live around Jake McBakery, you got to know where that point is. Dunnie's seen it plenty, and you know what I think? I think Dunnie wanted a beatin,' just as sure as you're standing there."

"Has he hit you?" Lee asked softly. Betty McBakery's face flushed again, but the tears went away as she rolled her eyes, took a deep breath, and then threw up her hands in mock exasperation and walked away to the window.

"Has...he...hit...me?" she said, pausing between words for emphasis. "Does it snow in the hills? Goddamn it, lady, he's hit me dozens of times. Until I learned to see it comin'. Dunnie's goin' to keep on gettin' hit too till he learns the same."

"Do you want someone to help you about this or not?" Lee asked in a matter of fact tone, keeping eye contact, but Betty McBakery was finished with the conversation. She returned to her chair near the window and relit the cigarette that had gone out in the ashtray. They stood silently until Lee spoke: "I need a phone."

After a minute-long pause that seemed like an hour, Betty McBakery led Lee down a hallway to the bedroom with the telephone. Dunnie's mother filled up the air with her cigarette smoke and bumped against first one wall and then the other as she grunted instructions as to how to find the phone. Lee positioned John and the officer in front of the door for privacy, and she remained inside for twenty minutes. When she came out, she announced she was ready to leave. Betty McBakery and Dunnie stayed closed inside the other bedroom, and the three of them left without good-byes. Once outside, officer Miles added that Mary McBakery really wanted Lee to come back to her house once she finished with Dunnie. Lee quickly agreed and got directions.

As they drove to Mary McBakery's house, John felt the return of all the old fears about being found out, but these concerns seemed a distant second to what had just transpired in the trailer park, and he could see that Lee had things on her mind other than his worries, so they sat silent for most of the ride.

John reflected on having seen yet another side of his cousin, the doctor side, and he silently marked his admiration for her skill and patience with the boy, especially considering that she had no doctor's bag of instruments but still found a way to give him an exam. Finally, John found a question that he thought would be received: "What do you think will happen now…with that situation?"

"The Child Protection Team will be out there first thing tomorrow morning," Lee replied matter-of-factly.

John went further with his question. "Gosh, do you think that will really happen? I mean, with the way that policeman was talking. I'm not sure they will…"

"It *will* really happen because they know who they are dealing with!" Lee interrupted John with a loud and aggressive comeback. "This is not my first spin around the race track. I got the right people on the phone, I know the right things to say, and *they will* be out there tomorrow morning or I will know why!"

John backed off from his questions and just looked at Lee, her face flushed and angry, her hands strangling the steering wheel. In the next moment he saw tears in her eyes, and she pulled over to the side of the road and into a dirt driveway that seemed to go no place in particular. She put her face in her hands, and the first words came out softly—"I did not come out here on my day off"—before she completed her sentence with a scream that shook the car: "*to get involved in this kind of shit!*"

"This was my first full weekend off in a month!" she continued. "Why can't I just have a nice quiet time in the country with my car? Why does the whole damn world have to be taken care of, and why do I have to be the one who does it?" She was pounding the steering wheel with both hands.

Lee switched off the engine and turned to John with a rapid-fire monologue. "Would you like to hear what I've been through this month? All I wanted was a little peace and quiet after going through hell." She took a deep breath and continued. "I had to turn off a respirator on a seven-year-old girl three weeks ago. Me, the goddamn intern, and I had to be the one to do it. Not the attending. Not the senior resident. Me!" Lee was speaking more slowly, looking right at John, not exactly accusing him of anything but making him squirm by the story she was telling.

"I'm the lowest piece of dirt on that whole team, and they dumped the shit of turning that machine off on me. Oh, sure, they did all the talking to the family and were huddled with the chaplain and prayed and all that incredible crap, and then they turned to me and said it was my job to actually do it."

The story poured out and rolled over John. It was beyond his experience, and he could do little but listen in silence. "This girl, Tracy, had tuberculosis meningitis. It took so long to figure out what was wrong. All the tests…and she went into her coma…all the tests took so long to come back that by the time they figured out it wasn't your garden variety thing, she was basically brain dead." John was able to offer a few clumsy words of comfort, mostly by remarking that he had no idea about the things that doctors went through in their training years. Lee accepted his attempts as genuine and appreciated the effort and continued.

"But you want to know the damnedest thing?" Her words came out fast and with her emotion rising and falling, at one moment angry and at another with a needy, almost pleading tone. "When we turned the respirator off, she didn't die. She started breathing just fine on her own. Had enough brain function left to breathe on her own...everyone was stunned...especially the family that had gone through this awful thing...agreed to let her die and then she just kept on breathing. And you know what, through a lot of this, I kept thinking, damn it, I have about fifteen other patients to take care of that are going to walk out of here, and I don't have all this time to spend on one patient, who we still figured would never wake up, but the family wouldn't let me leave. They wanted more and more out of me. I just don't have that much to give and now this...this damn kid and his fucking busted nose and fucking busted glasses. *This shouldn't be my problem!*"

"So let's just leave," said John.

"No," Lee shot back, "we do need to have a talk with Mary McBakery," and she started the car.

# Chapter 5

# Generations

## At the old McBakery homeplace

Mary McBakery became an orphan in 1920, sometime before the age of ten, and was placed in the Sermon on the Mount Home for Children in Halifax County, North Carolina. No one knew her exact age because she entered the orphanage simply as Mary Wallace, with no written documentation of her birth and nothing that clarified whether she had a middle name. She could neither read nor write and did not speak for months after she was placed. The unnamed people who delivered her to the orphanage said that her parents died of beriberi. She later came to understand that this was a vitamin deficiency that occurred most often when people took most of their calories from liquid spirits of one sort or another. Despite ultimately becoming the unofficial historian for the family into which she married, she never made any attempt to find out about her own parents.

In the early part of the twentieth century, there were a number of orphanages across North Carolina. Sermon on the Mount had a unique history in that it was not founded by a church or organization as were the Baptist Mills Home in Thomasville and the Oxford Orphanage run by the Masons, for example. It came about through the remarkable efforts of one man, Chester Penbry. He was a self-educated and self-styled evangelist, and he pursued a vision that he said was based on the lessons of Jesus's Sermon on the Mount. He preached that the material goods we find plentiful around us are sufficient to sustain life if we are willing to share what we have, regardless of how small or insignificant our portion of earthly goods is. What we give away comes back.

He succeeded in convincing churches of several religious denominations to work together, and he had an uncanny knack for getting people to give him money, materials, and their labor. Each spring and fall of the year, he conducted outdoor spiritual revivals that would run non-stop for days. During one of these, he was seized by the Holy Spirit and would or could not stop praying. He chased after people who tried to leave the revival and followed some of them into their homes. Ultimately, people became afraid of him and the authorities locked him up in the state mental hospital in Raleigh.

When he came out of the hospital, however, rather than being rejected and shunned, he was welcomed back by the local people as a visionary, and he gathered around him a small, devoted group that helped him achieve his dream of founding an orphanage. The main orphanage building took the shape of a cross with the arms housing girls, the base housing boys, and the head of the cross serving as the dining hall. As the numbers of children grew, other buildings were built and different age groups had their own dormitories. Then came school buildings and more than one hundred acres cleared for dairy cows and other farming used to support the orphanage. The number of boys and girls of all ages grew to more than five hundred at one point, and Sermon on the Mount prospered, becoming a virtual city unto itself, even more so than the other orphanages.

Chester Penbry's chief assistant was a man that everyone called "Grandpa." Mary McBakery never actually knew his name. He did everything for Reverend Penbry. He kept financial records, supervised building construction, and served as the primary contact for people who wanted to send children to the orphanage, among other duties. As time went on, Chester Penbry more frequently was unable to calm himself down, and Grandpa became a sort of brother's keeper to him.

Mary Wallace first saw Grandpa when he came to the dorm late one night to have a counseling session with one of the girls. He took the girl down the hall into the office, and they stayed there for over an hour. When she came back, she was crying. Grandpa commonly selected girls to counsel in the late evening hours, usually just one girl out of a particular group. Mary McBakery once confided in another girl how jealous she was that these other girls were getting extra attention. The girl told her to shut her mouth and that she didn't understand what she just said, but she still felt that maybe there was something wrong with her that she was never chosen. Another girl told her that she was too old, that Grandpa liked to work with girls of a very specific age, and when they grew older, he no longer had an interest in them.

Mary remained at the orphanage until she was fourteen, when Sermon on the Mount burned. It happened when nearly the entire population of the orphanage was celebrating with an athletic field day a few miles from the campus. There were only two girls who did not attend the field day, left behind sick in the room that passed for an infirmary. The main building and all of the dormitories appeared to catch fire simultaneously, and the only structure that was not heavily damaged was the one housing the infirmary. The girls were not harmed and said that they slept through the entire tragedy. No one was injured.

Sermon on the Mount Home for Children was never rebuilt. By that time Chester Penbry's episodes of madness were coming more frequently, and he no longer had the energy or the following to continue. Soon after the fire, he admitted himself back to the state hospital, where he died several years later.

There were a number of theories as to why someone burned the orphanage. Chester Penbry had become vocal about admitting children of all races to his facility, and for a brief time there were whites, blacks, and Native Americans sleeping in the same buildings and sitting in the same classrooms. It was no secret that there were people in the community who felt this was not right. Other people thought it was the two girls who started the fires, but still others thought that the arsonists simply saw them there and spared the building where they slept.

Mary McBakery then moved to the Oxford orphanage, where she became known for taking care of other people, and she soon caught up with other students in schoolwork. She stayed until she was twenty-one. She was fighting those in charge who insisted that it was beyond the time for her to leave when Louis McBakery proposed marriage to her in 1931. Her wedding was the event of the season in Oxford that year and took place on the campus, under a grove of magnificent oak trees. More than one hundred orphan girls of all ages, all in pink and blue, served as bridesmaids.

Grandpa showed up just before the wedding and asked her if he could give her away. She gave him a very public no, saying that since she had never been owned by anyone, there was no need for her to be given away. This was a side of Mary McBakery that few had seen up to that point but one that Louis McBakery and others would soon come to know.

Such were some of the experiences that influenced Mary McBakery, experiences unknown, of course, to John and Lee Randt as they drove to her house following their encounter in the trailer park. The roller-coaster events and emotions that John had experienced over the last few hours had rendered him somewhat numb, and he was making peace with the danger that they may yet be found out as imposters. This seemed almost irrelevant now, but he did wonder what specifically was on Lee's mind, so he found the voice to speak. "I'd really be interested in what went on the first time you talked with Mary McBakery. I mean it might help me to understand what's getting ready to happen now."

Lee quickly glanced at him and gave an expression that led him to feel he was simply an irritation to her, but she took a deep breath and replied, "OK, that's only fair, but the truth is nothing very much happened. I walked to her house—it's just on the other side of the cemetery—she gave me some tea; she talked about herself. I thought I'd get twenty questions about who I was and who my relatives were, but it wasn't like that at all."

Recalling the description of Mary McBakery by the man named Billy, John had assumed Lee would get a grilling about who she was, but Lee insisted to John that Mary McBakery seemed mostly like a lonely person who was looking for a friend, or at least someone to talk to. Lee explained that despite what she had said about it not being her job to take care of the whole world, she was going to see the old lady out of courtesy, not out of intent to set her straight.

Out of the corner of her eye, Lee saw John shake his head and heard him give a sigh that betrayed his confusion. She said to him in a neutral but mostly friendly manner, "John, you and I have known each other for just a few hours, and you don't know me and I don't really know you, but I think you need to not be so afraid of people. She's not dangerous and nothing is going to happen here that's going to be a problem. Just relax and deal with them." None of this quite made sense to John, and he had no reply to his cousin as they pulled into the driveway at their destination.

Mary McBakery was standing in the yard, tending some flowers, when they arrived, but she turned her attention to them promptly. She waited patiently while they parked the car and greeted them with a pleasant smile. Lee was out of the car quickly and went immediately to her. "Do you know what we found out about Dunnie?" she asked. Mary McBakery replied that she did, that the officer had called her on his police radio with a basic description. She also added that this was not a surprise to her.

"Not a surprise?" Lee started, then backing off from an accusatory tone and adding, "Well, I just hope someone can give this family some help and maybe part of that is for Dunnie's father to spend a little time before a judge."

"Jake McBakery has spent a little time before a judge, and a little time in prison," the older lady replied with just a hint of rebuke in her voice to Lee, who stopped speaking and waited for her to continue. "But if you want to hear…I mean if you really want to talk about this, and I will if you want to, let's go inside and sit while we do it." With that she turned and walked slowly toward the house, setting aside her tools and removing her gloves.

John did not comment, but he was surprised at the appearance of the house. It was a split-level brick ranch. He had expected an old Victorian house or at least a farmhouse more in keeping with the style of the church, but this was a modern home and not very old.

Once inside, Mary McBakery did not stop in the living room where she and Lee had their visit earlier. She continued down a long hallway to the back of the house, moving past a wall of pictures that seemed to span several generations. John thought to himself that at another time, and in another family perhaps, he would have a hundred questions about who was on such a wall and about the stories the pictures could tell.

They stopped in front of a set of large matched doors, ornately carved and not in keeping with the design of the rest of the house. With real effort the older woman put her shoulder to the doors, which swung open with a low-pitched creaking sound. John and Lee stood still, astonished. There behind the double doors, inside the modern brick ranch, was what remained of an old farmhouse. Mary and the rest of the family had given up on trying to repair and maintain the original homeplace, but they had preserved much of it and incorporated it into part of the design of the new house. Large, rough, exposed wooden beams supported a twelve-foot-high ceiling, and a sculptured ornate mantle surrounded a fireplace large enough for an average-sized person to stand inside without stooping. Old blackened cooking pots hung from iron posts within and outside the fireplace, and some old fashioned blacksmith tools were prominently displayed.

The two guests stood for a moment without moving and then accepted the invitation to sit on a red velvet couch flanked by matching chairs with large comfortable arms. Their host busied herself with preparing a pot of tea in another room just off this thirty-by-sixty-foot-long great room into which they had come. Mary's bed was at the far end of the room, and some of her clothing was displayed on wire mannequins placed as carefully as in a window store design. A large wardrobe beside the bed served to set off that end of the room as a separate space. Between the two ends of the room, filling most of the space around the walls, were an antique lamp collection, chairs, desks, potted plants in large vases, and other pieces of furniture. John thought to himself that the arrangement of the items was not cluttered or crazy in the way that he knew some older people hoarded meaningless relics; each piece was placed with order and taste and without the uncomfortable feel of a museum. This was a home. The order within it helped John to relax and feel more comfortable than he had felt since leaving the airplane.

With the three of them now seated for conversation, and following some polite interchanges about the presence of such treasure within an ordinary-looking house, Lee pursued the topic of Jake McBakery: "I…I…uh…just would like to know that the young man I just saw could get some help…some safety. But you were going to tell me about Jake McBakery being in prison. Was it for child abuse?"

"No, it was for manslaughter. He was drinking and went over to the wrong side of the road and hit a car. It was ten years ago and he spent three in prison, most of it here locally, in the jail, let out to work and all that."

John commented that even though it was a terrible thing, he knew of other situations like this in which the drunk driver did not spend anywhere near that amount of time in jail. "What about the man that he killed?" asked John.

She explained that it wasn't a man he killed. It was a whole family with three children, a family that had money and influence, and there was no way that he was not going to go off for a while. She proceeded to explain that if she named the family, Lee and John would certainly recognize the name, but that some things were best forgotten and she was not going to bring up the past.

"Digging up the past is a risky affair," she concluded. She said those last words in a way that led John to long for more information, but he couldn't find a way to ask a question that sounded appropriate.

Lee tried to redirect the point of their conversation, commenting, "Mrs. McBakery, I do have compassion for people with alcoholism, but that's not really my point here…"

The older woman ignored Lee and continued her story as if there had been no interruption. She seemed compelled to tell about Jake McBakery himself and the tragedy that happened right after Dunnie was born. She described the family with two children, Dunnie and Bennie. She spoke in a manner that seemed rehearsed, like she was telling a story that she had practiced and presented many times.

"Now Bennie was the golden child, but Dunnie, there was something wrong with him when he was born…didn't come home from the hospital with his mother. I don't really know what it was. And Jake was upset and started drinking. He loved that older boy, but somehow with Dunnie being…uh…some kind of damaged…he just couldn't get involved with him. Jake and Betty were having terrible fights about it."

At this point Lee felt it was pointless to either interrupt or continue the conversation about this with Mary McBakery. She had hoped the older woman would be an advocate for the child, but instead she was more like an apologist for his father. When Mary McBakery paused her monologue, Lee made a few general comments about hoping that everyone in the family could get some help, and the three of them sat in silence for a time.

John broke the tension with a comment that he hoped would carry the conversation in another direction: "I noticed all of the old pictures on the wall. They seem to cover many generations."

Mary McBakery pursed her lips, smiled, and then sighed, "You know a lot of people think that I know all about all those pictures, but the fact is that I am pretty much an impostor in the McBakery family."

Lee had just taken a drink of her tea, and had she not finished swallowing, she would have it sprayed across the room in response to the older woman's comment about being an impostor. Instead, she choked on the tea as it went down and spent a few moments coughing and clearing her throat. This diversion also kept John's expression from notice until finally Mary McBakery explained what she meant.

"Indeed, I did marry Louis McBakery, and he and I had mostly wonderful years. But beyond him, I don't think I was ever welcome in this family. And I wasn't the only one. Winnie Callum married Jackson McBakery, and she was one that did have fire in her belly for family history." Mary McBakery told how the other woman "went snooping around and found out some things that this family did not want to know about." Mary continued, "She was called a liar to her face by more than one person when she tried to tell what she found. She was working on a book about the family tree, but with all the criticism from others, she finally gave away her papers and disavowed any involvement with McBakery family ever again. She and her husband Jackson moved away to West Virginia, and she never finished the book."

Mary McBakery saw the look on John's face and read it correctly, saying, "And what she found out I will never repeat. End of that story." She continued, "So because I was married to Louis and because we lived in the old homeplace, I get to keep all this McBakery family trash and family treasure, and Lord knows, sometimes it's hard to know the difference."

John picked up the thread of the conversation. "We met this man named Billy who seemed to think that you were the family historian. He said you knew all the stories on all the people."

"If I do know anything, it's because of my work, not because the McBakery family confided in me. I worked for the Red Cross in this part of the country, and I traveled around, from Raleigh to the foot of the mountains west of here. Actually, a lot of McBakerys worked for the Red Cross. One of them, woman named Ella, actually worked with Clara Barton as the Civil War was winding down."

"Clara Barton? Lee and John said simultaneously.

"Yes," replied Mary McBakery. "I suppose that her name is pretty much unknown unless you have a reason to know it. The founder of the American Red Cross, that's Clara Barton. And it's been kind of a tradition that most every generation had somebody working as a nurse or for the Red Cross. I always thought it sort of a payback for all the blood that the McBakerys spilled; only fair that some of them should be gathering it back up again. You do know that's what the Red Cross does, don't you?"

The older woman's tone had gradually changed as the conversation progressed. She was more animated, even a little preachy to her guests now. She pointed her finger in the air and told them that she wanted to finish the story of Jake McBakery and his troubles.

"Jake McBakery got out of jail for good in 1975, and everyone was happy for a while. Jake was sober, and he was spending time with his boys and especially Bennie, who he called 'little Jake' even though that was not his real name. How he loved that boy. And then in 1977 when little Jake was riding with his grandfather…he had gotten real close to his grandfather when Jake was in prison and still spent a lot of time with him…they were both killed on the railroad track."

John interrupted with how he knew about this wreck and told of meeting Stanley and going through the junkyard, and the two women listened impatiently for him to finish so that the story could resume. Mary continued with a description of how Jake McBakery "went more than a little crazy" when Bennie died. Jake blamed his father. He blamed God. But mostly he blamed himself, thinking that if he had not been away, his son and his father would not have been spending so much time together and would not have been on that railroad track at that particular time of day.

Jake McBakery withdrew from the world and would not talk to anyone. On many days he sat beside his irrigating pond, trying to get enough courage to swim to the bottom and never come up. But mostly he just cried. And screamed. He yelled so loud he lost his voice. A number of people tried to speak to him, but he threw rocks at them and chased them away. He cleared out a little space in the tall grass near the wood line and slept there for a month. Betty and Dunnie would take food to him but wouldn't get close to him. He stayed that way until he got back in his truck and had another wreck. It was a clear attempt to kill himself, but he survived. When he came out of the hospital, he went back to some version of normal, but anyone who knew him before could tell he was different.

John could tell that Lee had reached a saturation point with all of this, but he was still interested in the stories. Mary McBakery too could sense that Lee was uninterested, and the two women stood up with the intention of ending the visit. John interrupted with a question that he intended as supportive but that he knew could be an invitation for more. "I guess this family has had more than its share of tragedy."

"I suppose that some would say so," she answered, and she then directed them across the room to the mantle and pointed out a set of pictures hanging above the fireplace. "Here's the saddest story of all, and maybe it was something that got this family going in the wrong direction. You know the Bible says that the sons will pay for the sins of the fathers."

She pointed out the portraits of two young boys and proceeded to tell the family story that everyone knew. "These are not pictures; they are drawings, of Adam and Joseph McBakery. When they were about nine years old, they just vanished. They were out in Colorado where William Bess McBakery was trying to get rich in a gold mine or something."

She continued the narrative about how Will McBakery left to go find them and was never seen again, or so the story goes, and about how Sarah returned to Virginia, remarried, and became known as the "Eve" of the family. She explained how every one of the McBakerys at the reunion was related to Sarah. The pictures of the missing boys were created by an artist in Asheville whom Sarah hired; the artist used a pair of local boys who resembled Sarah's sons to make the paintings, which were the only images were ever made of the children who disappeared in 1873.

Mary McBakery explained that this story was the one that got Winnie Callum McBakery interested in family history; Winnie "paraded it around" in the newspapers and gave talks about it in the local library to people interested in history. She traveled to California but never found a single person with the McBakery name. Winnie Callum had even come up with an idea to make a movie about the disappearance of the boys, but most people thought that was beyond what the story deserved and were growing tired of her obsession.

At that point in Mary's story, a car pulled into the driveway. Officer Miles gave a short blast on his siren, and the three of them went to the door. A man was in the back of the police cruiser. It had to be Jake McBakery. Mary went into another room of the house and did not go outside, but Lee marched directly to the police car. John walked away to another part of the yard. He did not hear and he did not ask about what happened between Lee, the officer, and Jake McBakery. Lee's only comment was that finally someone decided to do something about a problem. As they walked to the car, she did not want to talk about it. She said that it was time for them to go where they were supposed to be going and that she had done enough taking care of people for a while.

# CHAPTER 6

# SECRETS

**In a Civil War cemetery, Kittrell, North Carolina**

As it turns out, Mary McBakery had decided that she was not ready to end her visit with the new members of the McBakery family. When the police car drove away with Jake McBakery, and Lee and John were walking back to their car, she came out of the house, purse on her arm and floppy red hat on her head, with a large piece of chocolate cake wrapped in tinfoil. She announced that since "problems" were over for the moment, she would like to get to know the two of them a little better and have some fun. With a spark in her eye and a bounce in her step, she declared, "I get so tired of messing with that McBakery family. They can just take care of themselves for now. Let's go on a trip. I'll show you one of the prettiest places on God's green earth."

Lee and John looked at each other and laughed. They realized that any chance of meeting up with the real family was pretty much gone. It was almost four o'clock now, so there was time for one last episode in this whatever-it-was of an afternoon. Mary McBakery was delighted that they said yes and handed them her possessions to hold as she went around the side of the house for her vehicle. "I'll drive!" she added excitedly as she disappeared around the corner. John was finally and fully into the adventure. He put her floppy hat on his head and made a silly face.

The older woman came around the corner driving her 1979 Ford Ranger pickup. The words "Lariat V8" on the side of the front fender announced additional bells and whistles, including exceptional engine power. "What is it with these women and horsepower?" John silently thought as he buckled himself into a more traditional seat belt, expecting another version of off-to-the-races. They sat up high, riding on oversized tires, but Mary McBakery drove carefully, keeping to the speed limit at all times. She said she would go slowly so that they could look at some pictures she had pulled out of her large purse. John asked her if this had been her husband's truck, and she said without elaboration, "No, this is my truck."

Soon after getting underway, Mary McBakery told Lee to pull out the pictures she brought. In one of them, Mary was dressed in what looked like a nurse's uniform, but she explained that this was her Red Cross uniform and proceeded to tell a number of stories about wrecking her car while driving through a storm to help some people during the great polio epidemic of the 1940's. "I guess you young people have never heard or thought much about that kind of thing; it was pretty much under control by the time you came along, with your shots and everything."

John became aware that this conversation was becoming mostly a dialogue between the two women, so he just stayed quiet and listened and looked out the window. "But that's enough about me and the Red Cross. You're in training to be a doctor. I want to hear about that," the older woman remarked with genuine enthusiasm.

Lee paused for a few moments before answering and then began slowly, "Well, you know, that thing you said about being an impostor?" John felt a brief moment of panic again, thinking that she was going to confess their deception, but Lee meant something else entirely. "Most days, I'm operating under false pretenses myself, putting myself forward as a doctor. I mean I'm working in this hospital, surrounded by other doctors of all training levels down to medical students, and most of the time the patients don't know who is who, so you have to introduce yourself…and when I say, 'I'm Doctor Randt,' some of them look at me like, 'Who is this little girl?'…or that's what it feels like."

Having been jerked awake by the fear that Lee was going to tell the older woman the truth, and wanting to find a way back into the conversation, John asked, "How many women were in your medical school class?"

"Twelve, out of a hundred and twenty," Lee replied and continued, "and you know I think all the professors and deans tried to steer us all into pediatrics. It's OK for a woman to be a pediatrician, but not much else. Or she can be a shrink."

"Is that not what you want to do?" asked Mary McBakery.

Lee paused again and waited before speaking, as if making up her mind about whether she wanted to talk about this. When her answer came, it came out full of emotion and nonstop, the energy level of it rising as the story unfolded: "Actually, the very, very best experience I had in medical school was when I did a two-month rotation in this hospital emergency room in Tarboro. The doctors down there were busy...and I think a little bored with some of the routine stuff...so they let me do all the stitching up of the little cuts that came in. God, was that fun! And there was this one little boy who came in with his finger cut completely off and I helped the surgeon sew it back on...and it took. He actually saved that little boy's finger! And I was part of it!"

Lee was becoming more animated, almost bouncing up and down in her seat. "And then there was this time...Jesus this was amazing...in the middle of the night, this man came in with a bullet in his chest, right next to his heart. The surgeon let me scrub up with him and stand beside him while he opened the man up, but it turned out that the bullet had made this tiny hole in his heart, and when the surgeon pulled the bullet out, blood shot up to the ceiling and all the way across the room every time his heart pumped. So the surgeon took hold of my finger and stuffed it into the hole and said to keep it there until he could get some things ready to sew it up properly. So I just stood there for about five minutes feeling this man's heart beat around my finger and feeling the blood rush past the tip of my finger. But it worked! It was amazing! I didn't sleep at all that night. Didn't even think about rest or food until halfway through the next day, after the man was in recovery and things got routine again."

"Gosh, child, I think you need to be a surgeon, not a baby doctor," said Mary McBakery.

"I went back to my advisor after that because it was time to pick what kind of internship I was going to do, and he told me he didn't think that was really such a good idea. One of my advisors told me this joke about orthopedic surgeons. You know what qualities you need to be an orthopedic surgeon? You have to be strong as a bull and twice as smart. I laughed at his joke, but what he was really telling me was that I didn't have what it took to be a surgeon. It took a man."

"Poppycock," came Mary McBakery's one-word reply.

"I do regret that I didn't pursue it, at least pursue the discussion with my advisors. Whether or not it would have made a difference, I wish I had told them how excited I got when I got to look down into someone's insides and what satisfaction you get from stitching up flesh and then watching it grow shut and heal. But you know, I worried that if they knew how much fun I had doing it, they would never let me near it again." And with that she laughed a little demonic laugh that caught Mary McBakery up in the moment.

"Let's cut up some men!" Mary McBakery cackled.

"And then sew them back up again!" answered Lee. John kept quiet and looked out the window.

"But here's why I dropped it," Lee went on with the story "I think about how much I feel like I'm operating under false pretenses now, calling myself a doctor, and that's on a pediatric residency. I mean...what would it be like being the only woman on the team? I'd be treated differently one way or another, and not in any way that could be good. Like the day that we were learning about how to do prostate exams, and all the men were doing them on each other, and the women were sent into another room to use these plastic models...how stupid is that!"

"That may be a little more than I need to hear about," put in Mary McBakery, with a tone that was part real and part false modesty.

The conversation paused then until the older woman broke the silence. She told Lee that this "impostor thing" they both had in common was a thread that ran through her life. She related the story of her years growing up in the orphanages and of her marriage to Louis McBakery,

"He was a good man; and he did love me more than anyone has ever before or after, but the truth is, if I had had anywhere else to go, I would never have married him. That's a lot of what it was like for a woman in my day, especially one that was an orphan girl." Then the conversation died, and they rode along in silence.

They were finally at their intended destination. Mary McBakery gave them a brief history lesson about the town of Kittrell. It was once known as Kittrell Springs, a place where wealthy people came to bathe in hot springs and be healed of what ailed them. When the springs dried up, so did the town and little was left. The few houses and buildings that remained had evolved into a college for a brief period, and the college was now a government-operated job-training program. But just on the edge of town was a Confederate cemetery that had consumed much of the older woman's interest and energy over the years. It was said that Clara Barton had tended some of those who now lie there. Partly out of a wish to be connected to someone or something in the past, Mary McBakery had made the restoration of the cemetery her passion.

The driveway into the cemetery was lined by towering crepe myrtle trees just now coming into their full green growth of the season, still several months away from the promised display of red. The graveyard itself was a combination of a large modern private section and a small historic section clearly set off from the rest by a border of tall cedars on three sides and a small ornate metal fence on the remaining side. Mary McBakery pulled up to the parking area and proceeded with a history lesson about Clara Barton and the soldiers. She took Lee's arm and directed her around to survey the graves. John counted one hundred and twenty white marble crosses, ten rows of twelve. Each marker was approximately two feet high and aligned perfectly with the others. Four of the crosses were marked as unknown, but all the rest listed first initial, last name, rank, and company.

Just then, a small car pulled up beside the truck and a man got out. John heard Mary McBakery make a false groan and explain that this was one of the local caretakers of the property, and no one could walk into the historic section without him noticing from his house across the road. "He's a nosy, unpleasant man. I wish to God I had never asked him to take this on," she said in a loud whisper before steering Lee away to the far end of the older section.

The man greeted them cheerfully—"Hi there, Mrs. McBakery, how you doin'?"—but the women had already walked away, leaving John to speak with him alone. The caretaker was dressed in old denim coveralls over a bright red flannel shirt that hung out on one side, giving him a rumpled look. "I'm Jenkins, the main yardman for this place. I see you're here with Mrs. McBakery. Any particular grave you're looking for?"

"No…uh…I guess just the soldiers," John replied, somewhat distracted by some of the man's features, including the unlit cigar tucked into the side of his mouth, which did not perceptibly alter his speaking, and the top of what looked like a whiskey bottle wrapped in a brown paper bag protruding halfway from a pants pocket.

"So you're not from around here?" the man continued while pulling out a few hand tools from the front seat of his car and leaning them up against a tire. He was a muscular man with large dirty hands, and John watched him flip his hatchet a complete rotation in the air and catch it without looking at it.

"Well, I'm in town for the reunion," John went on, aware that this was the first time he had actively participated in the lie.

"So you're a McBakery?" With that question the man gave out a mischievous little laugh that made John laugh too.

"My wife is." John lied again and was surprised at how easy it was to continue the made-up identity as long as people bought the first part of story.

"So sweet ol' Mary is telling stories again, is she?" The man was asking these questions as he went about his business of organizing his tools. It seemed to John that he had come with a purpose and not just to check out the visitors.

"I guess…I mean yes…she's giving us a history lesson or two."

"But is she going to tell you the whole story? Are you some of the people who get to hear the real story that nobody talks about? Or do you get the sweet and proper story of the great lady Sarah McBakery and all her descendants that were fruitful and multiplied and inherited the earth?" As he completed his sentence, he laughed, a bit louder this time. He laughed hard enough that he lost his balance for a moment and had to grab the open door of the car to steady himself. John could see that he was more than a little drunk.

John was, of course, intrigued, and even though he reminded himself that a genealogical search in this family had no real meaning for him, he couldn't help but encourage the man to explain what he meant by the "whole story" as opposed to the "proper story."

"OK, then grab that little ax and follow me." The man named Jenkins led John around the side of the enclosed Civil War grave sites and through a grove of hardwood trees crisscrossed by well-worn paths that had been cared for with some effort; they included some white marble gravel but were mostly made of dirt. Beyond the path, occasional patches of grass alternated with kudzu, its greenish brown tentacles of new growth just beginning to reach out. On the other side of the hardwood grove was another section of the cemetery. In contrast to the other parts of the graveyard, the care of the graves there was spotty. As few as half of the twenty-five burial sites showed any sign of attention. Some of the headstones had fallen over, and some were ancient stones that had lost all discernible engraving some time ago. None had new flowers; a few had withered wreaths from seasons ago.

"This is where the bodies are buried," said Jenkins, attempting some wordplay that John actually understood, but John tolerated the man explaining the double meaning of his sentence. "This is where the great lady herself, Sarah McBakery, lies today." They stood in front of a marker that was much newer than the date of death recorded on the polished granite.

Sarah McBride McBakery
Wife of John Phillip McBakery
1844–1910
Mother of Us All
Walks with the Lord

John stood for a moment and looked at the area and offered a few observations. He noted that there was no marker beside Sarah McBakery, but there was clearly a space for a grave with the ground sunken in at a depth of six or so inches. He also commented on the newness of the headstone.

"Ha!" barked the caretaker with obvious glee. "You're one of those people that goes around digging up stories about people. You're a damn troublemaker, and you want me to tell you the whole Webster's unabridged version of why that headstone and the body that used to lie beside Saint Sarah ain't there anymore. Aren't you, now, aren't you…tell the truth." The man was drunk and happy and delighted with the opportunity to relay what he knew. He stretched out a dirty arm to surround John, but let him go when John caught a scent of his breath and other measures of hygiene and pulled away.

They each took a seat on nearby toppled grave markers, and Jenkins rolled out his story. He retold the story of the disappearance of the two boys in Colorado, giving John no opportunity to say that he already knew that much. He reviewed Sarah McBakery's return to Virginia and then to her move to North Carolina, where she married her dead husband's brother and started "populating the earth, or at least a goodly portion of western North Carolina," as Jenkins described it.

He leaned in close to John and added, "But here is where it gets interesting. Her husband didn't die—the guy out in Colorado, he wudn't dead!" Jenkins cackled, emphasizing the last part of his sentence with a joyful dramatic flair and exaggerated southern accent, somehow turning "dead" into a three-syllable word.

"Will McBakery finally made it back to Virginia about a year after Sarah married his brother and found her there with another set of twins in her belly that belonged to his brother. And see…nobody knew this, or was willing to say it until Winnie Callum married into the family and decided she was going to do everybody a big favor and write a book about the McBakery family."

Jenkins would tell part of the story, wait just a moment to see if John understood so far, and then continue, laughing and smiling all the time. He explained that he was a schoolteacher and librarian and helped Winnie Callum with some of her research.

"And you know," he continued, changing his narrative to a more reflective tone, "if she had just stayed in libraries around here and stayed there in Warren County, there would never have been a problem. But she had to go up into Virginia, where Will, John, Sarah, and Ella came from, and she found Will McBakery's grave, with a date on it fifteen years after Sarah married John."

"Ella, you mentioned an Ella," asked John.

"Yes…so you don't know about Ella." Jenkins was still excited and animated but looking a little tired. "I think have the energy to tell all of this…Ella was John's first wife…who also died…in childbirth…and left behind a child. But when John and Sarah hightailed it off to North Carolina, they left that child behind, and people in Virginia knew about it and were more than happy to tell nosy little Winnie all about it."

"I think I'm getting this down," put in John. "So Winnie, who is writing the history of the family, comes back from Virginia telling them about how Sarah's marriage to John isn't exactly on the level, plus there was this unknown child in Virginia…"

"Right!" announced Jenkins with renewed joy at having an audience who seemed to understand and was actually listening to him. "Winnie came back from Virginia and told the things she had found out, that the marriage between Sarah and John was not legitimate. She told the whole damn McBakery family that they were a bunch of bastards!" Jenkins laughed until he almost fell down and then added, "Which they are, most of them…but not because of anything Saint Sarah did…they all end up being bastards on their own terms in their own way…nasty, nasty bunch of people."

Hearing these kinds of stories, John delighted in his own little heaven. It mattered little anymore that this was not his family. This was the kind of thing that Dr. Kingdon had told him about, the secrets and conflicts that craft a family identity. He knew that someday he would dig into his own family in just this way. He continued his questions: "Sooo…what about the empty grave beside her—was John McBakery ever buried there"?

"Brilliant!" shot back Jenkins. "I think you might know more than you let on…do you?"

"No, I'm just trying to put two and two together…"

Jenkins interrupted with more information, but admitted that here was where he got a little fuzzy on the details. He did not know why John and Sarah ever ended up buried here in the first place. But he did know that there were two very distinct groups of the family. The ones around Warren county and as far down as Durham County, were poor as dirt. And the others, the Asheville McBakerys, had all the money.

"See, John got in working for some banks, and if you know your North Carolina history, there was big, big money in Asheville before the stock market crashed. I mean big money. Vanderbilts and those kinds of people. But anyway, the way I understand it, is that this little cemetery here was supposed to be some sort of national shrine to Clara Barton, the Red Cross founder. The mountain McBakerys had all this money that they were giving to the Red Cross, so the momma and the daddy of all these descendants were buried here. Kittrell was still supposed to be some sort of resort for rich people and Clara's shrine would be right here."

"But then the stock market crashed and the hot springs dried up…" John filled in the blanks.

"You get it," said Jenkins, "you're a quick study, young man. But the shit didn't really hit the fan until Winnie came back with her big discoveries and people started calling her a liar to her face. She finally just left. And then these people came down from Virginia...and here is where I get fuzzy about all this...with a court order to dig up the grave and take John back up to Virginia where he was born. Just him. Not Sarah. Best I can figure the girl...it was a girl, I recollect...that John left behind in Virginia in 1876 had some relatives that got all stirred up and decided to bring daddy home to be buried beside Ella. And as far as I understand, that's where he is today, beside his first wife."

"Now that's a story for the ages," John commented, shaking his head.

"I'm almost done," Jenkins cut back in, finishing the story of how the "mountain McBakerys got all hot and bothered" and decided to move Sarah's body back to Asheville. And then Louis, Mary's husband, finally got everyone together and convinced them to move her back. This was why the headstone was so recent; the old one had been moved so many times that it broke apart. By then the nastiness of the McBakery bloodline had been diluted enough for people to quit fighting over caskets and dead bodies, as Jenkins understood and explained it.

"By the way, the caskets of John and Sarah were something to behold; they died before the stock market crashed and they had funerals that went on for days...caskets worthy of a parade through the streets of heaven," came the last bit of information from Jenkins.

Jenkins's narrative ended on that note. John silently relished all the new images to which he had been introduced in the course of a day: first, modern-day Jewish wise men rushing down to the medical center to see Jesus and now a parade of golden caskets through the streets of heaven.

Jenkins walked away, to work or drink or both, and Lee and Mary McBakery came back down the path toward John. They stopped and motioned for him to come to them. Mary McBakery was obviously not interested in this other graveyard. The sun was near setting and they were losing the light. Mary McBakery said she did not like to drive after dark, so they needed to go.

The day was finally over. They drove back mostly in silence. John wondered what things had transpired between the women while he was hearing secrets revealed. He felt a sense of satisfaction in knowing these stories and felt no need to retell them for confirmation or otherwise from Mary McBakery. He felt a sense of excitement and adventure about what lay ahead in his own family.

# Chapter 7

# This Can't Be My Real Family

### Next day at a cousin's house

The next morning, John awoke on the couch in Lee's apartment and found that Lee had left for morning rounds at the hospital. As he cleared out the morning mental cobwebs, he had a fuzzy memory of a dream of Joe Cocker singing "Feelin' All Right." As he later learned, it was not a dream. Lee's routine at four o'clock in the morning required loud music for motivation to actually get her out of bed and over to hospital rounds. She would play an upbeat rock tune and dance around in the apartment, getting up her courage to go "impersonate a doctor." That morning she kept the volume at half the usual level, and John slept right through it.

To his surprise, John found a note giving him permission to borrow her car to drive back out into the country to visit one of the people he should have met the day before. Lee knew the way to this house and left him a detailed map. He felt that her allowing him to drive her car was a real act of trust, and he actually did some stretching exercises in the parking lot before getting in the car. He wanted to make sure that he was ready to handle this car in a safe way. He knew how to operate a stick shift, and after a few slow test laps around the parking lot he headed out onto the highway.

He drove cautiously and without incident except for coming on an accident that held him up for a few minutes because the gas tank on one of the damaged vehicles had ruptured and was spilling fuel on the road. There was a fire truck blocking John's way, hosing down the spill. The report of the wreck served as a good icebreaker when he got to his destination, in part because the son of his father's cousin was the assistant chief of the local fire department and would surely have been one of the men on the truck. He was to come over later if he could get away.

Unfortunately, the sharing of information about the wreck served to be the high point of the visit. They went through the usual chatter about the definition of first and second cousins and the "once removed" designation and then found little else to talk about. Soon into the conversation John thought to himself that he was about as welcome here as the tax collector. A local comparison might have been the preacher who invited himself to dinner. John tried the usual opening questions about how who knew whom, and who lived where when, but what he got was always a one-word or short-phrase answer.

Ultimately the son arrived, and indeed, he had been at the wreck; the conversation about that filled up another ten minutes. John's second cousin Mark, the assistant chief, seldom looked at him. Most of the time, his attention was focused on what was in the refrigerator, and for a good part of the time, he actually had his head inside the refrigerator, leaning down and looking long and hard at whatever was there, with his backside pointed at where John was sitting at the kitchen table. John made a few attempts at a more personal dialogue with the son, talking about his school program, about Lee, and about his parents, but no follow-up questions or information from the others was forthcoming. At one point the conversation fell quiet for more than a minute, the silence broken by the mother of the house asking, "Would you like for me to fill that tea glass back up?" John declined. At this point he didn't want to have to go to the bathroom a second time, but it did occur to him that maybe if he looked in their medicine cabinet, he would a least learn something about these people.

He made one last attempt to find more informative common ground by asking if they by any chance had any old pictures of his father, perhaps at family gatherings when his father was a child. This family had none and even had difficulty recalling exactly when they had last seen John's father.

Back in the car, John had the rest of the afternoon to just drive around in the warm spring countryside. He used the time to try to put into perspective this most recent bit of the roller-coaster ride of the last few days. Failure to make any sort of connection with the cousins left him sad and hungry for something he could not quite name. But the experience with the other family reminded him that something could happen. He told himself he needed to be patient. He met Lee for a late dinner since she was not on call, and he was somewhat revived by her energy. She had learned to perform circumcisions that day and told John far more than he ever wanted to know about the procedure.

Lee drove him to the airport for his evening departure flight, but it was delayed and he had time to sit in the terminal and watch the people around him. He saw a three-year-old win a power struggle with his mother while the father stood by passively instead of helping. One of the flight attendants, a tall athletic man with oversized shoulders and a wristwatch with three time zones on the face, intervened with a toy for the child. John watched a friendly red-haired man about his age deal with the boredom of the wait by striking up conversations with other passengers, and he admired the man's ability to relate to strangers. That's what Lee would do, he imagined. She would never just sit here; she would make something happen. He tried to think of something that he could do rather than just wait, but then the announcement came that it was time to board.

By the time he took his seat on the plane, his enthusiasm and his determination to continue this family search had returned. There were people to meet, events to attend, and secrets to be discovered. He had Dr. Kingdon to guide him and the example of a new friend to maybe help him be not so timid.

# CHAPTER 8

# A COLORFUL LIFE

## May 1981, San Francisco

John Randt finally had time to open the letter from his professor containing his end-of-year evaluation in his favorite class. He knew it would be a good report, and he valued the opinion of this teacher, so he saved it until he had time to really read it. Until now, he had been busy preparing for the trip to San Francisco, where he had landed a summer internship in the program of his choice.

He read the first words of the evaluation: "Thank you, John, for the most colorful presentation of family dynamics that I have ever seen in a classroom or anywhere else." John put his head back and laughed one of those out-of-control sustained bursts of laughter that makes a person's sides ache.

"Colorful?" he said out loud to only himself, "colorful?" This was certainly the first time in his life that the word colorful had been applied to John Randt. Smart and successful? Yes. Hardworking and dependable? Certainly. But "colorful?" This was new.

In fact John's classroom report on the exploration of his family's secrets, which he had passionately and methodically conducted over the last year, had the class of twelve students holding their sides with laughter and crying real tears, all within the space of twenty minutes. This presentation was a sort of "final exam" for the advanced family dynamics course under John's beloved Dr. Kingdon. He was one of the last to present, and up until then, no one else in the class had paid much attention to him. If they thought about him at all, they saw him as a quiet, serious student who at times annoyed other participants with how much he quoted the family therapy gurus of the hour.

This end-of-class presentation was designed to allow the students to describe their efforts in finding information about and moving to some understanding of the family in which they grew up. Most of the presentations were deadly dull, some given by neurotically tortured young people. One man cried when talking about his father who had abandoned the family. One of the presentations was even more painful. A young woman revealed her own childhood sexual abuse, despite clear guidelines from the instructor about what kind of information belonged in the course and what belonged in personal therapy. The student then started shaking and said she couldn't breathe and had to leave the class.

John chose to give his presentation in a manner that was more akin to a stand-up comedian's style, warming up the crowd with his father's corny jokes, such as "How many dead people are in that graveyard?" The answer? "All of them." How often dad told the joke, every time they passed a cemetery, was offered as the real punch line, and John's audience started to chuckle. The trip with Lee to the reunion had them really laughing.

Then John revealed the interaction and the story coming from it that led the students from laughter to tears. He told of having dinner with his parents. While some comfort had returned to his visits home, his parents were resistant to revelations of any meaningful degree. Most of their dinner conversations were still about John and his plans and accomplishments, if they were personal at all. His mother's contribution to the dinner dialogue lately was usually something about what cute thing that Dusty the cat had done the night before. But at a key moment during this particular dinner, John reached over and took his mother's hand, looked her in the eye, and said, "Mom, I really do love your mashed potatoes, and I do really care what Dusty did last night, but what I would really love would be to hear something about your life before I came along."

John had not expected the class to explode in laughter, and professor Kingdon was surprised as well, but this difficulty in getting information that John was describing, this longing for connection that all of the group participants carried in them, was so universal and so powerful that they all welcomed the opportunity to release the emotion in any available manner. Laughter was safe.

What John's mother then told him took them in another direction. She didn't come right out with it, and she went to great lengths to make sure it was acceptable to John's father that she reveal it. The story concerned the engagement of John's parents, at age eighteen for both of them, just after graduation from high school. Six weeks before the wedding, she had lost the engagement ring that John's father had given her. Certainly John's father had been upset, but not simply at this single event, because there was another layer to it, having to do with John's grandparents.

Going back another generation, John's father's parents had had little money when they married, and they had accepted the gift of a set of rings to use in the ceremony. The rings came from several generations before, and this was the third or fourth ceremony with them. The rings were not so very valuable except in their legacy. Some years into her marriage, John's grandmother had taken off the rings and placed them in a cup beside the kitchen sink. John's grandfather then came in, ran himself a drink of water from the tap, drank most of it, and then tossed the rest of the water, and the rings, down the drain. A substantial amount of water had gone down the drain before the couple realized what had happened, and by that time, the rings had passed through the trap and into the sewer system connected to an underground septic tank.

John's grandparents were furious, each blaming the other for the greater stupidity. She blamed him for the act of throwing the rings down the drain, and he returned the anger fourfold for the act of putting them in the cup in the first place. John's father was six years old when this happened and recalled being terrified by the fight between his parents. It went on for days. Ultimately the grandfather decided that he would dig up the septic tank and get the rings back. He was not a happy man as he dipped through the sewage of the tank, one bucket at a time, pouring the family's human waste into a strainer, searching for the rings. He cursed so much that mother and children went to live with relatives for most of the long weekend that the father toiled. The rings were not in the tank so he decided to dig up the sewage line that led away from the house, and there he found both rings trapped in a rough spot in the line, two feet from the house.

This event did not end the marriage. The emotion of it was managed through a silent mutual vow to never speak of it again. John's father had banished it from his consciousness, until his bride-to-be lost the ring he had given her. She tried to hide the fact that she no longer had it, but he kept asking why she did not wear it. When she confessed to her carelessness, he was enraged. Driven by emotion, the memories, and the inner demons from the prior ring incident, he broke the engagement. Despondent, she married someone else within the year, and he followed suit. It took each of them a year apart from one another to realize their mistake. They divorced and finally married each other, this time using the antique rings thus passed down to yet another generation.

John told this story to his class with the skill of a professional storyteller. He could not explain how he had developed this skill, except to say it had developed out of hours of reflection about both the story itself and the manner in which it unfolded, told by his mother, who ended the story in tears in the arms of her husband, who held her closely as she wept without shame or control. John looked on astonished, first by the display of emotion and then by what he ultimately labeled as the "privilege" of seeing the interaction between his mother and father and of knowing all this about his parents.

When John told the story to his class, he described the grandfather's time in the septic tank in a way that confirmed the preposterousness of some things in life. The laughter from the students went on and on. When he described his mother's tears, his audience plummeted back down into genuine sadness. His classmates and Dr. Kingdon sat spellbound when he talked about what he had learned from this. For him, this story "helped the universe make sense." The orderliness of his upbringing was not a random or arbitrary feature of his life. It was training given by his parents to enable him to "escape the consequences of careless behavior, not to mention the dangers of intimate relationships," in John's own words.

Dr. Kingdon never doubted that John was a good and capable student, but John's presentation moved him to work hard to find John a summer internship worthy of a "truly thoughtful student," as he described him in the evaluation that John read that first day in San Francisco. Dr. Kingdon helped him secure a placement in a clinic just north of San Francisco that specialized in family therapy. John was told that it wouldn't be unusual if one of the "giants" in the field, Murray Bowen, Peggy Papp, or Harry Aponte, spent time at the clinic that summer.

San Francisco was an ideal place for John to be for a second reason. His father had a photograph of the brother of John's great-grandfather standing on the tree stump of what looked like a giant redwood that had been cut down. It was a faded black and white picture of a team of men posing for the camera, apparently showing off their accomplishment. Although the family held on to such photos and knew that a family member was posing in one of them, the full story of where and what they were about had been lost. John's father told him that if he wanted a family mystery, he should try to find out what this was all about. The fate of the man in the picture was also in question, and any West Coast Randt descendants were unknown.

John took the picture to the university library, knocked on the door of several history professors, and finally tracked down what was almost certainly the location and topic of the picture. He found out about William Carson, the northern California man who was the first to figure out how to cut down a tree of that size and bring it to market. He learned that in Eureka, California, today stands a remarkable mansion that Mr. Carson built using the wealth of his timber-harvesting enterprise and the marvelous redwood itself. John collected and reviewed enough literature and tourist brochures about the Carson Mansion and redwood-timber-harvesting in the area to convince himself that the picture of his great-grandfather's brother was taken somewhere in northern California.

John thus had two plans for the summer: to sit at the feet of the masters of family therapy and to search for the missing ancestor. He was new at this kind of investigation and hardly knew where to begin. He learned that in California most old records were centralized in the state capitol and that various fires and calamities had destroyed a lot of information from the era in which he was interested. But he figured that there must be some information available locally as well, so he identified six county seats and made plans to visit each place. He vowed to himself that if Randts had ever lived in northern California and had married, had children, paid taxes, bought land, left a will, or been arrested or hanged, he would find out about them.

So it was with high hopes for both of his summer tasks that he arrived for his first day in the family therapy clinic. He walked into the large two-story Victorian house that housed the clinic, stopping for just a minute to survey the lush gardens that spread around the grounds, and introduced himself to the receptionist. She looked at him without speaking, walked away, and said something to another woman seated behind the reception area. The second woman, named Carrie, greeted him in a friendly manner and said the staff was excited about his being there. After about twenty minutes of orientation conversation, John asked Carrie about the apparent cold shoulder he had been given by the receptionist.

"Oh, that's just Beth. She's going through a phase now…she's not speaking to men at this particular time," replied Carrie.

"Uhh…doesn't that kind of get in the way of her doing her job?"

"She'll get over it…we're a very accepting group here; there's lots of diversity here," Carrie explained to John. He didn't quite understand what diversity had to do with it, and to him it seemed more like an issue of common courtesy, or of doing a job. Just then a tall man with long hair and a beard walked by wearing a long gray robe. Carrie saw John's eyes widen and proceeded to explain.

"That's another example of what I mean. That's Rondahl; at least that's what he wants us to call him now. But his real name in Benjamin Gibbons."

"Rondahl?"

"He's taking a new name. He says the three-part names that we all have now are derivative of our identities that come from others. He says he's trying to 'define himself.'" Carrie emphasized the last two words by making the quotation mark sign with her fingers. "He's actually got a lawyer working on the papers to legally change his name."

"Is he sticking with Gibbons for a last name?"

"Nope, just one name, Rondahl."

"So...he works here?" John asked and Carrie replied that Rondahl was one of the therapists. John's eyes widened further in the next hour of Carrie's introductions to and descriptions of others who worked in the clinic. She explained that he would be working in "*the* eclectic clinic" on the West Coast, that there were places with better-known names, such as the Eslen Institute, but that if you were looking for a place that presented real dialogue and discussion by the best in their fields about the differences of opinion about what you do to help people, then this was the place. Carrie defined herself as "conservatively trained" and indicated that most of her work was administrative in the clinic. She said more than once that she loved the atmosphere there, but that you had to keep an open mind.

John still had one more question about Rondahl. If he wanted to have an identity not defined by any predecessor, was it not a problem that he looked a lot like Jesus? But this was John's first day in the clinic, so he decided he would wait until later to ask.

Following the half-day of introductions, Carrie led John to the large auditorium, a recently built modern facility connected to the back of the house. She explained that today was the day for "Grand Rounds," a weekly gathering of all the students and teachers at the clinic. Today there would be a presentation by a psychologist named Rita Holland-Hill. Carrie conveyed real enthusiasm for what was to come, explaining that Dr. Holland-Hill always led the group through fascinating discussions of human behavior. John was bold enough to ask Carrie what Rondahl might think of someone with a hyphenated name, one that must be derivative of much meaning. Carrie responded that Dr. Holland-Hill and Rondahl were great friends and that if John wanted to know Rondahl's opinion about this, he should ask Rondahl directly.

Rita Holland-Hill presented the case of a seriously depressed woman and the child for whom she was unable to be an effective parent. John thought the family sounded a lot like Betty McBakery and Dunnie. Dr. Holland-Hill approached the problem with a history lesson about marriage as a "property arrangement" that no longer worked for women and concluded that unless the woman in question would enroll in her group therapy for "consciousness raising," there was little good that could happen.

When the presenter finished the sentence that contained the words "consciousness raising," a middle-aged man in an expensive-looking three-piece suit exploded out of his chair and exclaimed, "Consciousness raising? Consciousness raising? What a piece of malarkey!"

The man moved out into the aisle, indicating to the audience that he had considerably more to say about the matter. John understood some of what the man said about psychological theories of development, but he was generally lost as to the points the man was trying to make. But the man was clearly angry and critical of the woman Dr. Holland-Hill described for what he defined as the woman's decisions about how to live her life, and John remembered his concluding statement: "the only way to raise this woman's consciousness is to grab one ear with one hand, the other with your other hand...and pull as hard as you can!"

Neither Dr. Holland-Hill nor anyone else in the room reacted with much surprise to these comments. Carrie whispered to John that this was the usual kind of response from Dr. Raymond Sorrow, a psychoanalyst who worked in San Francisco and who spent a few hours in the clinic each week. "I don't think he has a lot of women patients," added Carrie quietly to John.

At that point Rondahl stood up and announced, "I have something to say." He did not go ahead and say it immediately, but instead stretched himself up to his full stature, looked around the room to make sure everyone was looking at him, folded his hands in front of himself as if in prayer, and then slowly began. "It is all a matter of ego. And it is not about healing the ego, for the ego can not be healed; the ego must be given up."

John understood this about as much as he understood the analyst's theories, and he took a quick look at Carrie, who leaned over to him with, "That's mostly what he says these days. He's not quite got it worked out how you're supposed to give up the ego, but it's what he talks about all the time."

Someone else stood to speak, but Rondahl interrupted him with a gesture of his hand: "And I'm not done. I have more to say." Again, he dramatically surveyed the audience for their readiness to hear. "And it does so appear to me that before this sad lady can be able and willing to give up her ego, some of us here in the room must present her a model, and we are so far away from doing that." With that he made an exaggerated turtle-like stretching of his head and neck, pointing his head first at Dr. Holland-Hill and then at Dr. Sorrow, and then he smiled, looked around the room once more, and sat down, appearing pleased with himself.

Others spoke but John remembered little of what they said. He wondered what kind of place he had signed on to. He looked down at his schedule for the rest of the week; it listed face-to-face meetings with the cast of characters he just had seen in action. As the group filed out, having settled little about how best to help the depressed woman and her child, John remembered that this was a paid internship that would last six months, and his father had told him that he would help him to buy his first car. His thoughts turned to that practical task and to the trip he would make this weekend or the next to a destination north of San Francisco, in search of his missing ancestor.

# Chapter 9

# Another Roadside Distraction

**In a new Honda, north of San Francisco**

It took John the better part of a month to actually get his car, since his father insisted on a particular model. During one telephone discussion John pretended to have his heart set on a 1980 Pontiac Firebird with a V8 engine and listened to a five-minute speech from his father as to why this was not a good idea. His mother, who was listening in, knew John was joking, but they both let Dad go on and on and then ribbed him in a good-natured manner.

It took even longer for John to get on the road north of the city. The internship was structured in a way that did not yet allow him weekdays off, and he was becoming impatient to conduct his family search. So one Saturday morning, knowing that no government offices would be open, he got in his Honda Civic anyway and drove up the coast of California. He realized that he would not just go around a corner and see a road sign that said, "THIS WAY TO THE OLD RANDT PLACE," but he wanted to do something, so he was on his way. He also wanted to see what a real redwood tree looked like, and he wanted to stand on the trunk of such a tree that had been cut down, as his great-grandfather's brother had done.

He drove north on Highway One. He enjoyed his new car, even without a big engine, and he used the time driving up the coast to digest all that he had been through in the last month in the clinic. Several of the people who at first seemed bizarre—clearly more than simply colorful or "diverse," the word Carrie continued to invoke when things got strange—had turned out to have a practical side when it came to the actual work with troubled people. The angry psychoanalyst and the therapist who looked like Jesus sounded more alike in how they thought about personal misery when John heard them speak individually and in small groups, away from the arena where everyone gathered to debate ideas.

John was glad to have this time alone to think. He drove slowly that Saturday morning, taking in the scenery of the California coastline. It had a different look from places he had been before, and he felt no great hurry to get anywhere. He passed through several small towns, and just north of Anchor Point, he spotted an antique store that looked interesting. The sign on the well-kept wooden building said, "GOLD MINE ANTIQUES." In the mood to stretch his legs and browse, John pulled into the parking lot and saw displays of old picks, shovels, and wagon wheels, lots of wagon wheels. Inside the store were smaller items including old pans that were used directly in streams and guns, knives, and hats, some of which looked like they might be old, but some of which were clearly modern knock-offs that might have been made in Japan. The more closely he looked at things, the more he saw a lot of plain, tacky tourist items included among the real treasures.

He looked up at the wall where there was a display of old advertising signs and a lot of liquor and saloon signs, including some that might have been real and some that were clearly reproductions, and in the corner he saw a skillfully carved wooden sign that made his mouth drop open. He read it twice to himself before he really believed it. It read "A. R. McBAKERY MARCHANDISE AND GENERAL GOODS." He approached a man who was minding the store and asked first whether it was genuine, and second whether he knew the story behind it.

"It's legit," said the man, adding, "it's a nice piece, nice wood, nice work. That store operated about halfway between Mendocino and Eureka for a long time. Notice the word 'merchandise' is misspelled. In the antique world, that adds a little to the value. Good woodcarver…not a good speller."

"But what about the name, McBakery, do you know the story…"

"I wouldn't, but my wife might. Charlotte, want to see if you can answer this man's question?" he yelled across the store to the woman on the other side.

John talked with the store owners for about half an hour, interrupted occasionally by other customers. The owners knew almost nothing about the man whose name graced the sign. They thought he had died long ago, but they did know the man who ran the store after him; first, they said it was A. R. McBakery's son, but then they remembered that the man's name was Griffin, so their best guess was that it wasn't his son, but might have been his son-in-law.

"Buster Griffin was some kind of relative. I think he married McBakery's daughter. Anyway…the way I understand it, it was a family business and it was McBakery's kin that kept it going, until Buster retired and shut it about ten years ago."

John was trying hard to remember the details of what Mary McBakery had told about the twin boys who had vanished. Could they possibly have made it to California and continued the family line? One moment, John was saying to himself that the last thing he needed was another adventure in the McBakery family, but in the next, he found himself caught up again in the mystery. It was simply too rich of a story to not go further with it.

John posed one last question to the woman who was giving him body-language messages that she had given enough of her time to someone who was not going to buy anything. "Is it possible that this Mr. Griffin has any relatives still around here?"

"Why don't you ask him yourself? He lives in the big rest home three miles up the road…at least he was still alive last Christmas. We helped move him there after his stroke. We bought out the rest of what he had in the store, what was worth anything."

John walked out of the store trying to put together all the possibilities. At best, a long shot by any measure, this man in the rest home, who John wasn't even sure was alive, would be the son-in-law of one of the twin McBakery boys who disappeared almost a hundred years ago. The opportunity to speak about this to a live person reminded him of one of the points Dr. Kingdon made over and over. He said you have to go talk to the old folks in the family. He said that in digging up information, you needed to talk to real people. Even if there was some sort of "magic spyglass to look through and find all the remaining records of your family" and even if you had every deed, birth and death certificate, marriage license, photograph, criminal record, and everything else about your family, you would still not understand how your family's legacy and family members' identities had developed; for that you needed live people. Dr. Kingdon charged his students to "knock on doors; don't hang out in libraries."

With Dr. Kingdon's exhortations ringing in his ears, John drove up the driveway of the Seacliffs Retirement Home. The facility was relatively modern, with the landscaping well-maintained and parking areas well-marked. He sat in the visitors' lot for a moment, thinking about just how to do this. He wondered what lie Lee might tell if there was any challenge to his wanting to visit this man, assuming he was still alive. He decided to pose as an antique dealer who was interested in items from the old McBakery store and who was told that Mr. Griffin could be helpful in determining what was available and genuine. He thought Lee would be proud of him for this one.

He walked up a long walkway to the entrance and noticed that despite being newly painted, it was a most unattractive square brick and cinder-block building with small windows. It sat on the back area of a large lot between two older wooden-frame houses. Lining the walkway were perhaps a dozen men and women in wheelchairs or other types of reclining seats, all tightly restrained with bed sheets or some other kind of binding. A single attendant moved among them, giving drinks of some sort of liquid through their straws. It was now near lunchtime, and another employee came outside to begin moving the residents into the dining area. Most of those John passed gave him some greeting, but some only stared blankly. Some had food stains on their clothes, but they otherwise looked well cared for. John felt discouraged. He hoped that if Mr. Griffin was still alive that he would be in better condition than those in this group.

Once inside the door, John identified a Mrs. Luther in her office and inquired into the presence and the health of Mr. Griffin. He was indeed there, and John's story passed the test. Mrs. Luther escorted him down the hall to a private room. The halls were filled with weekend visitors, and John almost changed his mind about the wisdom of this, worried that if relatives were visiting, he might lose his nerve. He also realized that he could always just tell the truth about who he was and why he was there, but then he thought that the deception might be more fun.

He found Buster Griffin sitting in a chair in his room, attended by a young black man who was helping him organize his lunch. John was encouraged to see that Mr. Griffin was dressed in street clothes rather than bedclothes and that the eighty-year-old gentleman promptly turned full attention to the stranger who had come into his room. "I can introduce myself," John said to Mrs. Luther and thanked her for her assistance.

"Well, sonnyboy...who are you?" spoke Buster Griffin, reaching to offer his hand.

John felt encouraged by this greeting and decided to tell the man the truth. Buster Griffin, it turned out, knew nothing of McBakerys on the East Coast, but it was evident that his mind was clear, and John became so eager that he began rushing the story and the questions.

"Whoa...now slow down...you need to set yourself down and let me eat. We got all afternoon to talk about all this...if you're a wantin' to know about old Adam McBakery, I'll be happy to oblige." John tried to remember the names of the boys. He thought they had biblical names but was not sure which ones.

The attendant laughed and commented, "Sure, he'll *oblige* anything for a price."

"For a price?"

"You don't know what you're got yourself into, do you? Mr. G. doesn't give anything for free...he's a businessman. What he's got, you pay or trade for," the attendant explained and then excused himself, saying he would leave the two alone to talk. Before leaving, he laughed and suggested that John watch his wallet.

"No, no...set yourself down, sonnyboy. I'm not a crook," Buster Griffin reassured as he took a bite of food. His hands were as steady as his mind, and despite the warnings, John was excited. Nothing yet indicated that this man was not who he was looking for. "But you know, a good deed does sometimes deserve a return," he continued. "Pleasure of your company is 'nough for me. What do you want to know?"

John sat back in a recliner beside the old man and told him the story of the McBakery twins. Buster Griffin eyed him carefully through the telling of it, patiently ate his food, and gave John some information about who he was. Buster Griffin married Adam McBakery's daughter, his only child, with the explicit agreement that he would join in managing the merchandising business. He talked for about ten minutes about the life he lived in the store but did not address the implied questions about Adam McBakery's background. John held himself back from jumping to the money questions about whether there was a twin brother and other such information.

Finally the old man yawned and seemed to drift away from the topic, and John wondered whether he was getting sleepy or was more forgetful than he seemed. Then Buster Griffin offered an undisguised bargain. "I tell you what...my mind ain't what it used to be, but I do my best thinkin' when I'm a sittin' next to the water on Taylor's Beach."

John had to smile in the face of this deal that was just so obvious and so clever. John believed the old man knew exactly what he wanted to know, but he was indeed going to extract payment for it. "So, I take it you don't get out of here all that much?" John returned.

"Oh, I get out just about the amount I want to," came the cool reply, "but a trip to Taylor's Beach is a bit of a treat...that just might be worth it for both of us." Buster Griffin had a devilish look in his eye and at the same time was closing up his dinner tray as if to leave and do something else. John knew who had the upper hand here—there was no question at all about that—and he had already made up his mind to take the man for a ride down to the beach if it was at all possible, but this bargaining was actually fun and he wasn't quite ready to give in.

"Well, I would like to accommodate you, sir, but I suppose there are rules and regulations about all this and I'm not sure that I would be qualified…"

"Blake, the guy just in here, he'll fix it all up," the old man quickly put in, a little too quickly, John thought. Perhaps he was showing some anxiety about being turned down. "Go get him. He'll be in the dining room," Buster Griffin ordered.

John found Blake the attendant in the expected place and convinced him to go back to Buster Griffin's room. On the way back to the room, Blake chuckled to himself and John accepted his laughter and knowing looks with good humor. Once in the room, the attendant's manner changed: "No way, Mr. G., you know the rules. He's not a relative and you don't have a paper that says you can go off with him."

"To hell with that. Whadda you want this time, you no-account worthless good-for-nothin' you…" Buster Griffin bantered with Blake with a tone that had some anger but also seemed rehearsed.

"Wait," interrupted John, "you mean there really are rules against me taking him out of here?"

"Like hell there are…I don't have no guardian and I sign my own checks…I go any damn place I please!"

"Well, on paper, there are rules," Blake explained in a serious tone. "But Mr. G. and I, see, we do have this legal arrangement. As an employee, I can take him out, and I can't really, legally, let you have him, but…"

"Name your price, you sorry bastard, and don't get me goin' any more than that or I'll call you somethin' you don't want to hear!"

Though John did not know it, this was the language of the closing of the bargain between the old man and the attendant. The price would be a two-dollar tip—a small amount of money to Blake—but to this old gentleman who had spent sixty years running a store and arguing prices since the Depression, it was a meaningful amount of money. For this "highway robbery" of a price, Blake would either take the old man for a ride or arrange for someone else to do it. The six children and seventeen grandchildren of Buster Griffin were not all that attentive to him—they had to be asked, and some of them even paid to take him out of the retirement home—and if he had his wish, he would never ask or pay. Even though Blake did not know John, he had good judgment about people, and just for good measure, he later did record his driver's license number and his license plate.

John was still not convinced he wanted to do something that was illegal "on paper." That old fear that things were a little out of control came creeping back, but he remembered the time with Lee and how that ended up all right. He also looked into the eyes of Buster Griffin and saw someone that was begging, in his own way, for a ride away from the retirement home, to a place that he obviously loved. John recalled the words of the police officer when he invoked the plea of Mary McBakery to Lee, that it would be an act of kindness to help the family out with Dunnie. This would be John's opportunity to make just such a contribution.

"Let's get goin'," barked Buster Griffin. Blake told him to hold on for just a few minutes—that he had a few things that he wanted to send along with him, and that he would not be going anywhere until he came up with the two dollars.

# CHAPTER 10

# EUREKA

## Up the northern California coast

Even while settling into the car with his new friend, John felt the need for more reassurance from the attendant that this trip was reasonable. Blake had put together a traveling bag for the older man and had placed it in the back seat without explanation of what was in it. John looked up at Blake from the driver's seat with the car engine running and asked one more time, "So you think all this will be...uh...all right to do...to go on this trip to the beach. No one will get in trouble?"

Blake leaned his hands on the top of the car and looked John in the eye, "Now...here's the full story. Mrs. Luther hasn't gone into a resident's room in years. People like me do the taking care of people like Mr. G. And I'm going to be here the rest of today and tonight. Fact, I'll be the person in charge and if someone should ask...and I can't imagine who that might be...I'll cover."

He looked at John for a nod of approval, received it, and continued, handing John a piece of paper, "Here's the map to Taylor's Beach; it's not called that anymore, but it's not a problem to find. In the bag is another change of clothes, and a lot of bedclothes and towels in case he has an accident."

"An accident?"

"A bowel or bladder accident. Probably won't happen, but you want to be ready. Got all the stuff you could ever need."

The issue of the bowel or bladder accident not being at all on his radar, John started to issue another statement of doubt, if not protest, but Blake kept talking: "And here is the last thing you need to know. When you get back tomorrow, don't come here; come to my apartment because I won't be here, but I'll run him over from my place. The address and the apartment number are on the paper with the map. You can actually see it from here, up on that hill behind you. And my phone number and pager are on it too, in case he dies or something. Oh...but don't get worried when he gets a little confused or wimpy late in the day—he's been doing a little sundowning lately...that means his brain sort of sets with the sun." And with that Blake slapped the top of the car lightly, told them good luck, and turned and walked quickly away.

John sat still with the car motor still running, trying to understand what he had just heard. When they get back tomorrow? Was that what he said? He opened the paper with the map, and as best he could tell, Taylor's Beach was about a four-hour drive north of the retirement home. John thought he was going over the hill to the coastline. All the information about towels and bedclothes and *call him if the old man dies* echoed in his head.

He looked over at his traveling partner, who had a grin on his face. He and Blake knew this was the plan all along. John took a deep breath and one more look at the big smile that deepened the considerable field of wrinkles on Buster's face, and put the car in gear. Buster gave a laugh of delight and said, "Let's make some time now; we'll only have a few hours of light on the beach as it is."

The old man turned out to be a good conversationalist. His mind showed little evidence of decline, and he was a wealth of information about Adam McBakery. He was also clever in that he was not about to reveal all that he knew, knowing that how long they would actually be out was up to the driver. John realized that he was going to hear the story in the order that Buster Griffin wanted to tell it, so he did not push him for information he was not ready to give up.

"Didja' ever hear of William Carson?" the old man asked.

John had, of course, and he relayed the story of his own family and the picture of the man standing on top of the redwood tree trunk and told Buster that he knew about the Carson Mansion in Eureka. Buster Griffin replied that those kinds of hats, boots, and work clothes worn by the men in that picture were the kind sold at the store he ran for workers of a later generation. He explained that the store started out as a supply stop about half-way between the San Francisco area ports and some of the places where timber was harvested. He said as far as he could tell, only two kinds of people got rich either in the gold mines or with all the tree-cutting: the people who owned the land with the gold and trees and the people who sold them the tools they needed to work either kind of treasure.

"Did Adam McBakery get rich?"

"Absolutely he did, and he hung on to every penny of it like it was the last drop of water on the earth."

"So if he was rich and you married his daughter, how did you end up in a home like we just came from?"

"Hah…there's the story…he skipped over his daughter and me and gave all his money to his grandchildren in some fancy lawyer-fixed-up trust fund. He made my children rich, not me. Might near ruined a couple of them. By time they was grown, they didn' have a need to work. All but two of 'em turned out to be these hippy-dippy artists—ran these shops where they painted pictures and made statues. Go through Mendocino and you'll find four or five shops that they and their children run, all put there by Adam McBakery's inheritance."

John was becoming more hopeful that his companion had some real information for him, but Buster Griffin was in high gear telling stories, and he was not going to be interrupted. "But I really ain't going to complain. I got the best part of Adam McBakery, his daughter. We were married for forty-nine years. What about you, sonnyboy? I don't see a ring on your finger. You got a girlfriend?" The next hour was about imparting wisdom to the younger man about courtship and love and about how his wife died, of breast cancer. He said she never got a checkup because she was told that she was immune to breast cancer because she breast-fed her babies. He told how he discovered the lump and how he still had the will and the permission to "you know, be touchin' her like that" at age sixty-five.

Buster Griffin's advice to John came in waves, but he said there was something John really needed to remember: "Now don't you be one of those people that get so busy you forget to get married and have children."

John tried again and again to steer the conversation back to his interests, but Buster Griffin insisted there was more to say about William Carson, "Because you see, this William Carson was so important to McBakery, and if you don't know about that story, you don't know what I'm going to tell you about Adam McBakery."

John listened to the oft-told legend about how William Carson was traveling in a ship off the California coast, heading to Alaska to look for gold, when he saw the magnificent redwood trees on the shore. When the captain would not stop to let him off, Carson jumped off the boat and swam two miles to shore and ultimately became the first man to figure out how to harvest that kind of timber. He built a vast personal fortune.

Buster Griffin told in exhausting detail his version of the Carson history and his meeting with one of Carson's sons. He said Adam McBakery knew the sons and became a regular guest at the Carson mansion, and Buster insisted that he had a story to tell and he was going to tell it from the start.

"I'm gonna tell it to you just like it happened 'cause I was there. You got to know that by the time McBakery was around, the tree-cuttin' operation needed supplies of all kinds. That's how McBakery, and the old snake oil salesman that helped him get started, came in. McBakery, he did most of his dealing with this foreman named Mills, but one day he was there...an' me too...my first trip up to Eureka with him...when Carson's son came sayin' his men were getting ready to riot down as the waterfront. Goin' to riot over pay. Wanted to know if they had any ideas as to how to whup them."

John could do little but listen to all the stories about wives, trust funds, hippie artists, and timber harvesting, but he was still looking hard for a way to ask a question relevant to his search, though he found there was no way in yet.

"And this foreman, Mills, he was scared. But Adam McBakery spoke up and said he didn't believe that anyone was going to whup that gang of men and he suggested that they pay off who they needed to pay off with just enough money to get the job done. He offered to donate either a hat or a pair of boots to any man that would go on back to work."

Buster Griffin went on to tell the story of how he, Adam McBakery, and foreman Mills went down to the waterfront, where the trees floated down to the ships, saws, and warehouses, and walked directly up to a large crowd of angry men carrying torches. They gave the men an offer of a shorter workday and other work-related changes.

Buster Griffin continued, "Overnight, Carson's boy became a hero to the workin' man, and nobody ever knew it but those of us that was there, but it was Adam McBakery that steered him in the right direction. The Carsons 'membered it and so McBakery's store got all the business it wanted. And one other thing, Adam McBakery was a regular guest in that house and that's where he learned to read and write. Up till then he couldn't read. It was the old drunk crystal ball gazin', healin' tonic-sellin' man that kept all the records. He died with a dead liver 'bout the time that McBakery learned to read. Old Adam probably couldn't have kept the store up and runnin' if he hadn't learned to read."

"That's enough," John interrupted. "Those are interesting things you're telling me, but I've just about figured out that you don't really have any information I really want. I'm turning the car around unless you got something about Adam McBakery having a twin."

"Did have a brother. Don't know if he was a twin. Saw a picture of him. Looked like him. Never met him. Could'a been a twin."

"What happened to him?"

"Best I understood, he got on a boat and went somewhere else. It could have been to Alaska. I heard somebody say he went on one of those boats to China. China had a lot of people coming here around that time. In San Francisco and other places. Boats went both ways. I think he got on one of them and never came back."

"Okay, now we are getting somewhere. That's good. So how about if you just tell me what else you know about how he got here, where he came from, all that. He must have said something."

"I'll do that, sonnyboy, I sure will, but looky here, we're not all that far from Taylor's Beach. I think a whole lot better when I'm out there next to the waves with the wind blowin' in my face. And you do want to see some redwoods, don't you? There…turn there…redwoods right down that road."

By that time the two men were close enough for Eureka to start showing up regularly on the road signs. The scenic Highway One, which meandered up the coast mostly near the shoreline, had turned back inland, becoming Highway 101. Buster Griffin motioned for John to follow a sign that said "Avenue of the Giants." They were soon so deep into a forest that they needed to turn on the car lights, towering redwood trees dimming the sun's rays at five o'clock in the afternoon. They stopped several times to stand below and marvel at the massive, soaring trees. John tried to imagine what it must have been like for his great-grandfather's brother to harvest these giants. He wondered how people could bring themselves to cut one down, but he also knew that was another time, long ago. He tried to reach inside and feel a kinship with his woodsman ancestor, but couldn't quite make it fit.

At length John noted the time, and Buster Griffin agreed that they needed to go directly to the coast if they were to have any time there. The older man tantalized John at this point, saying that the beach was where he and Adam McBakery had spent a lot of time and that everything there was to know about his father-in-law had been told to him on that beach.

There was no sign that said "Taylor's Beach," but Buster Griffin knew exactly where he wanted to go, and with good light still available, they pulled into a parking lot overlooking the ocean. John looked out over the sand and the water and saw literally hundreds of giant logs littering the beach. He joked that they were "drift trees" and asked the older man about them. Buster explained that trees were logged and floated down rivers and that inevitably some escaped out to sea, ending up on the beach. Timber was logged this way for many years, and the numbers added up. One could find these beached giants all along the coast around Eureka, Coos Bay, and points north and south.

John helped his companion negotiate a steep path down to the beach, and they took seats first on some of the giant logs and then, wanting more comfortable seats, settled into a pair of nearby lawn chairs that seemed to belong to no one in particular. Blake had packed a hearty snack for them, and they sat and ate and looked at the ocean. A score of bathers seemed determined to stay through the last light of the evening, and another group had strung a dozen or more kites on a long single line. A strong breeze from the sea drew the multicolored collection of fabric birds, fish, dragons, and other designs into a long graceful arc. Cars were stopping at the overlook above to take snapshots of the display. The bathers, kites, and setting sun gave John a feeling of peace unlike anything he had ever felt before.

Buster Griffin interrupted John's dreamy state of mind by announcing that he was true to his word, that he would now tell him all about Adam McBakery. But Buster looked tired and his words were a bit slurred, and he repeated himself measurably more than during the trip here. But he persevered: "That story…the one I told you about going with McBakery to confront those workers at the dock…I was just ten years old, then, and…well…McBakery was just as much a father as I ever had, though it was more like we was brothers, him a lot older, me just ten…and then I married his daughter…I did tell you that I married his daughter, didn't I?" John was a little worried; the man didn't look like he was ready to die, but he looked exhausted. John asked him about it, and the old man admitted he was usually asleep by the time the sun went down but was "then back up with it, mind you."

But the old man kept talking. "Here's what we would do when he got older. It was just when the war, the big war, World War II was going on. And McBakery hated that he missed the first one, and he had by all measures given the store over to me…I don't know how old he was…'bout seventy, I guess…more like eighty…but he knew the Japs were lurkin' in the water out there. It's true…Jap subs were all over that place. Big cities blacked out far down the coast…so…so…here's what he…and me…I was there too…would do…he got these big lights, big lamps, and he fixed himself up a generator on his old Ford, and we'd come right out here and turn on those big lamps and yeeeeellllllll…at the Japs."

"You would…what…why would you yell at the uh…Japs?"

"We were trying to draw their fire! See, we were tryin' to trick them into thinking we were the town and have them shoot their guns here on the open beach so nobody would get hurt."

"Did they ever shoot?"

"Naw...because they knew we were ready for 'em. What I really believe is that we kept 'em from even sendin' scoutin' parties on to land, 'cause we were ready for 'em. We had a plan that we'd fight 'em in the woods. We knew we wouldn'ta had their firepower, but, pow! We'd hit 'em and run. They never tried us. And it was Adam McBakery that set it all up. He was the leader. But we all did our part. Had a sentry system up the beach. Had a plan that if they ever did fire, we could turn off the lights they were shootin' at and turn some others on, confuse 'em, keep 'em guessin'."

Buster Griffin was making less and less sense, repeating himself, and simply rambling from one topic to another with little transition. John remembered what Blake had said about the old man's brain setting with the sun. It had been a long day. He looked out across the ocean at the sun that appeared to get larger as it dipped toward the water. He sighed. The stories were over for the day. He tried to put together in his mind what he had learned. Here was the son-in-law of a man that could have had the same name as one of the boys that vanished in 1873, and the man had a brother about the same age. How convincing would such a story be? Did Buster Griffin really know any more?

John decided to get up and walk down the beach while keeping the old guy in sight, who seemed to be going to sleep right there in the lawn chair anyway. After taking off his shoes and dipping his feet in the cool water, John returned to find two children, a boy and a girl, playing near Buster Griffin. John watched them sneak up on the sleeping man and point and giggle and talk in rushed whispers to each other. Buster awoke, and he looked confused and frightened as John spoke hello to the children. With a wave of his hand, he yelled at them to "shoo away" and leave him alone, although it was clear they had done nothing but look.

The boy ran away quickly, but the girl paused a moment and took a step closer, entranced by something about the old man. Even in the dimming light, John took note of the contrast between the faces, especially the eyes of the girl and the confused man. Her eyes were bright and energetic, the white the whitest of white and the color a sparkling blue. The eyes of Buster Griffin were mainly tired, half closed. He struggled to focus first on her and then on John. The girl looked at John and ran away. The exhausted Buster Griffin looked up and said, "I jus' gotta get some sleep."

Then John noticed what the children must have been talking and giggling about. Buster Griffin had soiled himself, lost control of bladder and bowels. John could see the wetness soaked through his clothes and could smell what had happened. He drew back in revulsion. He saw that the old man was now fully asleep and would be no help in getting back up the hill, and he had no idea how to handle the situation. He stood there as darkness was almost on them and then stepped back and forth, raising his hands in the air in frustration and looking around for help.

John ran up the hill to get the bag of things Blake had prepared, not sure what to retrieve that would actually help with this. When he got back, the two children had returned, accompanied by their mother. The children were overheard making fun of Buster Griffin's mess, and the good fortune beyond John's hope was that the children's mother was a nurse.

"I...uh...this is just a little out of my league. You see...my grandfather..." John opened with another little lie.

"Where do you live?" Asked the woman.

"Well...long way from here. We're actually spending the night in...ahh...one of those motels...just back down the road. We passed a whole line of them."

"I've got a little time to help, if you need it."

Nothing that John said in the next hour betrayed his true emotion. He was fed up and done with Buster Griffin, and they would be going back home as soon as the sun came up the next morning. But on the outside, he was humble and kind and gave his helper just enough information to show how much he cared about his grandfather and wanted him to have these kinds of trips out of the retirement home. Together they crafted a makeshift stretcher out of a blanket and carried the sleeping man up the hill. Within fifteen minutes, they were checking him into the motel, and John got his first lesson in bathing and otherwise cleaning up someone soiled from neck to knee with human waste. The proceedings became even more difficult when they awoke a fussing, fighting, and confused Buster Griffin, who cooperated not one bit with his nursing care.

With all his clothes stripped, Buster Griffin was wrestled and half-dragged into the shower, fighting every step. "I'm gonna give you a Buster Griffin right cross!" he said at one point and began recounting his days as a boxer. "It's a comin', I'm gonna bust you one! You meddlin' sons-a-bitches!" His voice was fading to a loud raspy whisper, but his anger did not let up. He had lost all comprehension of the people he was with, and he fought with all his strength to stop them from bathing him.

The woman helping John said very little but went about her business in a professional manner. John struggled with the smell and the sight of a naked eighty-year-old man, who was smaller and skinnier than he looked in his clothes. He was pure white, mostly skin and bone, with the large muscles of his limbs having lost their former mass. He had large tortuous veins near the surface of his skin, something John believed suggested considerable past vigor.

Buster Griffin still had some strength left, however, as John learned when he was looking away from the old man, trying to do this task with as little close contact, visual or physical, as possible. Buster grabbed John by the hair with his left hand and delivered a closed fist punch that glanced off John's forehead. Not injured, but stunned and surprised, John staggered backward as the woman struggled to keep the older man from falling. She scolded John for not paying attention to what he was doing and lectured him about being on guard when trying to make someone like this do something he didn't want to do. John quietly accepted her criticism as they finished up their task, put Buster Griffin in the nightclothes that came in his bag, and tucked him into bed.

All this made John even more determined to finish with this trip as soon as they could get going in the morning. As the woman left, she gave John her home phone number in case of trouble. John emptied the pockets of Buster Griffin's soiled pants and found a roll of fifteen crisp one-hundred-dollar bills. "Well, so you're not rich, but not so damn poor that you can't pay for this room tonight," John said out loud to the sleeping man.

It was well past midnight when John finally fell asleep, having been reviewing the events toward the end of the day, as well as thinking about all the new information he had learned. He couldn't help but wonder if there was really any more to be learned, but as he finally drifted off to sleep, he didn't care. He had had enough.

But when John woke up the next morning, standing over him was a fully dressed, fully alert, and cheerful Buster Griffin, looking none the worse for wear. "Are you ready to find out the truth about ole Adam McBakery?"

John was not happy to see him or hear this. "No…I'm not. Just as soon as I get dressed, we are going back down the road!" He was out of bed and into the shower in a moment. He dressed quickly and with intention.

When John came out of the bathroom, Buster Griffin was sitting in an armchair across the room. He was wearing dressier clothes than the day before, with red suspenders over a starched white shirt and a checkered green sports coat. He was clean-shaven, with neatly combed hair, and he held in his hand a small derby hat with red rim. Thinking that Buster looked like a leprechaun did mildly amuse John but did nothing to change his decision that this journey was over.

Buster Griffin interrupted the deliberate silence. "Well, I guess if you want t' walk away from the only livin' man who knows how and why Joseph and Adam McBakery made it through the desert alive, then I guess it's your choice."

John's mind raced. Joseph and Adam—those *were* the names Mary McBakery had said. Hearing them together now convinced him. "So you have known this all along and you've just been stringing me along?" He did not hide his anger.

"No. Not exactly true. I knew some of it. What you told me helped me put it all together. He never told all of it. Just pieces. I never knew where he came from, just how he showed up. But it all fits. Fits real good."

"So let's hear it."

"Can't tell you. Have to show you."

John was furious. "Here we go again! No. N-O...No! I won't do it!"

"Looky here, sonnyboy, I got you this far didn' I? You got to trust me one more time. If you and me can ride up to the Carson Mansion, I'll not only show you what will make you sure about this, but you can take the God's truth back with you in a brown paper bag. We're jus' thirty, thirty-five minutes away."

They rode along in silence for the first fifteen minutes, heading north to Eureka. It was John who broke the silence and said, "So now you're just not going to say anything?"

"I figured you'd heard enough of my junk. Plus I got nothin' more that I want. I'm happy to be walkin' one more time into that house, one more time to look at somethin' that I always wondered about, and now you helped me understand jus' what I was lookin' at."

"Well, if I promise—I think you know I'll keep my promise—that we are going there, can you give me a hint about what this is that we're going to see?"

"S'pose a little bit of explanation won't ruin the s'prise." Buster Griffin took a deep breath and moved immediately back into storytelling mode. "But you still got to see it to really know what I'm talkin' about. See...Adam McBakery...I told you that William Carson's son taught him to read...but he never really did learn much readin' and writin'. I mean, he was 'most forty when he started, but what he could do was draw. Had a God-given natural talent for drawin'. With the pencils and papers that Carson's family gave him t' learn t' write, he took to drawin'...drawin' these funny pictures."

John Randt was now following signs into Eureka and allowing Buster Griffin to direct him to the house known as the Carson Mansion. "The big house is now owned by some private club, but we're in luck: in the summer they open it for tourists on Sunday mornin', and I'm jus' sure we can get inside," the older man explained.

"What do you mean funny pictures?" John asked.

"Funny…like people with big noses and big open mouths and big heads and ears. They'd look like the person that was being drawed, but, you know, funny-like."

"You mean caricatures?"

"Whatever. Lots of the people that hung around the big house would have him draw funny pictures of their kids or of them. Paid him a little money. But he'd draw other pictures and one of these you gotta see. I never understood it till now…I think I understand it."

John Randt pulled into the parking lot of the most remarkable house he had ever seen, the William Carson Mansion, a Victorian-style house with turrets and spires and ornate windows and doors all dressed up with color and surrounded with flower gardens in full summer bloom. He dismissed his first thought—that it was like something out of one of his childhood Dr. Seuss books. No, that wasn't it. It was more like what you get when you build a gingerbread house out of redwood trees.

Buster Griffin looked at John and chuckled, "Yes siree, I see that look on your face, the same look ever' body gets first time they see this place. Some house, huh?"

"So you're telling me that Adam McBakery has paintings…uh…drawings in this house?"

"I'll show you," and the two men moved up the walkway to the house and joined the short line of early arrivals for admission to the house. The old man reviewed part of the story he had told John before, about how he was a ten-year-old boy who kept company with Adam McBakery and ultimately married the man's daughter. He said that McBakery, sitting with him on Taylor's beach, usually drunk, and sometimes crying, told him stories of his life that were given only under promise that no one else would ever hear them. "But I guess I'm about to break a promise."

The line had started to move, and Buster Griffin was filling in the blank spots in the story John had come to hear. The key was the relationship of Adam McBakery to the old man who sold healing tonic and told fortunes and who, when he grew tired of wandering, opened a store that passed to McBakery when the old drunken scoundrel died from an alcoholic liver.

As the line fanned out through the stunning ornate rooms filled with antiques, oil paintings, and more stained glass than any church John had ever seen, Buster

Griffin moved John past the various treasures and down a short hallway to a more modest sitting room with large windows and a view to the garden. On the wall above a rolltop desk labeled as William Carson's personal writing desk were four caricature pencil drawings.

"There, 'at's the one we came to see. Looky there, that's his signature in the corner." Buster Griffin was pointing at a "funny" drawing of a covered wagon with "California or Bust" painted in big letters on the side. In the drivers seat was a man dressed in a suit and top hat with dollar bills sticking out of his pockets and from under his hat. Seated on each side of the driver were two small boys, each drawn in caricature, each with his mouth open, one crying, one laughing. In the drawing, the wagon appeared to be suspended in the air over a mountain range and a river, with a desert stretched out in the background, littered with cattle skeletons and tall cactus plants.

"I never quite figured out what this was all about until you told me your part of the story. All I knew—which was what McBakery told me—was that Adam and Joseph McBakery were the old snake-oil salesman's boys and worked the crowds of customers, some foolish 'nough to believe the tales about the healin' tonic, others jus' wantin' the fifty percent alcohol."

The two men stood in front of the drawings and tried to fill out the story. Buster Griffin learned from a drunken Adam McBakery sitting on Taylor's beach that the boys were mistreated routinely by the peddler, beaten and made to drink alcohol to the point they would pass out.

John mused, "But if those two boys did somehow end up in that wagon, taken or kidnapped or whatever by that man, wouldn't they have told somebody, couldn't they have escaped...or something?"

"Maybe...but ya' got to 'member the times. Right after the Civil War. This part of the country was still wild...an' I think I 'member hearin' McBakery say his parents were killed by Indians. If that's what they b'lieved...if that's what they were told...maybe they didn't think there was anybody left t' go back to."

"I just can't believe there wasn't some way for them to get back to their family. I mean, it seems like they didn't even try."

"Well, you know...human race is a sorry lot. It's like you can take an old dog and beat the poop out a' it all day long and the minute you offer it a kind hand, it'll come scratchin' and sniffin' back t' you. I seen people like that. Seen lots a' women like that. Man give 'em a beatin' ever' night and there they are the next mornin' cookin' breakfast. And ole McBakery, he had a real loyalty t' the old drunk peddler, seemed t' worship him. And McBakery, he was one of a kind...ever' day he got up was a good day t' be alive, somethin' good 'round ever' corner. He told me his brother was jus' the opposite; nothin' was ever good 'nough or right. I'd say up there in that picture that the boy with the big mouth smile is Adam and the one cryin' would be Joseph. That's likely jus' how they came 'cross the desert."

Ultimately the men stood in front of the drawing long enough to believe they had gleaned all the information they could from it. John took note of another one that illustrated what looked like two boys trying to catch a terrified runaway horse that had a plow being pulled behind it. The boys were pitched high in the air, and there was a man in the picture bending over backwards, clearly laughing. There was a woman screaming at them with her mouth as big as the horse's behind with the word "stop" in a big colorful word balloon above her head.

"Got what you need?" asked Buster Griffin, and they retraced their steps back to the car with only a brief time to survey the other riches of the mansion. The older man explained that he was ready to go; he just wanted to walk into that house one more time before he died, and he wanted to get back to the retirement home because Sunday night was when the cute young girls from the church choirs came to sing to the old folks.

They drove directly back with one short stop for lunch and two more for bathroom breaks. Buster Griffin asked John to pick up the tip since he was short on cash. In the car a few more stories came out, but nothing to cast doubt on the truth of the discovery, and nothing to suggest a more specific fate for Joseph McBakery. They arrived as planned at Blake's apartment and roused him from sleep. John said his good-byes and thank-yous and warned Blake about the mess in the bag of bedclothes. Blake and Buster Griffin proceeded to argue about when and how Buster would be taken back to the retirement home, the old man accusing the attendant of trying to rob him blind and yelling that he was not going to put up with it.

As John moved toward the door, Blake asked him if there was anything else he needed to know.

"No…not really…we just had a nice drive."

The last thing John heard when he walked out the door was the sound of a baseball game on the television and Buster Griffin yelling, "Billy Martin, you are a goddamn fool!"

CHAPTER 11

# A Little More McBakery Mess

## Back in North Carolina

Before John went to bed that Sunday night, after delivering Buster Griffin back to the home of the attendant, he wrote a letter to Lee. He had been in touch with her from time to time during the year since their first meeting, and he had written her in some detail about his genealogical interests and activities at the clinic. He couldn't tell if she gave much attention to what he wrote, but he understood she was busy in her second year of learning to be a "baby doctor." Her rare replies to him were brief and mostly about getting together sometime in the future when they each had more time. He let her know that he had something important to tell her, but was intentionally mysterious about it when he suggested that they contact Mary McBakery with the "interesting" information he had.

As it turned out, Lee and Mary McBakery had been having their own interesting experiences that led them to get back in touch with each other in a meaningful way. It began when Dunnie McBakery was brought into the emergency room where Lee was working as on-call backup for the pediatric intern. This time, the child was not brought in for treatment of physical injuries. Instead, he was accompanied by social workers from the Child Protective Services Unit of the county to be evaluated for admission to the child psychiatric ward.

Since Lee had some prior history with and information about Dunnie McBakery, she inserted herself significantly into his care, despite the fact that in other such situations, the case would have been handed off promptly and completely to the psychiatrists. Instead, Lee followed his progress for the duration of his stay under the guise of his needing a pediatric consultant for his general health needs. This was somewhat legitimate, but not to the level of interest and energy that she invested in the situation.

Dunnie, now eleven, had become aggressive and disorganized as his school year ended. The social workers still checked in on him because of the trouble from a year ago, and at first they thought his father must have been mistreating him again, but good information proved otherwise. When Sandra Miller, his primary protective services worker, observed his classroom once, she saw him attack another smaller student, and he needed four grown men to subdue him and calm him out of a sustained temper tantrum that seemed to come out of nowhere.

He was admitted to the child and adolescent psychiatry ward, but contrary to what Lee expected, he did not become the darling of the unit. This was not the sweet, giggling boy she had examined in the trailer park the previous year. He was a foul-mouthed, oppositional child who stole food, told lies, and generally provoked everyone around him. On one occasion, he slapped a nurse in the face and ended up tied with restraints to the bed in the seclusion room. When he struggled and cursed, refusing food and water for twelve hours without slowing down, he was sedated.

Lee volunteered to act as case liaison to his family and the Child Protective Services social workers, and though a few saw her involvement as unusual, most were so busy with other cases that they were glad to have her involved. She called both Betty McBakery and Mary McBakery and spoke with a number of teachers to get what information might be useful.

During the time that Dunnie McBakery was at his worst in the hospital, several family meetings were held with the doctors. Sandra Miller attended these and gave very positive reports about the work that Jake and Betty had done with her over the last year to try to provide their son with what he needed. Some of this had to do with the results of a psychological evaluation of Dunnie McBakery that was performed shortly after the incident the prior year. The tests found him to be much more capable than his parents believed him to be. The psychologist emphasized that the child had a normal IQ and, for the most part, negligible problems with learning skills, and he was more than capable of learning how to run a farm, which happened to be the only question Jake McBakery asked during the report of the evaluation. With this information the father seemed to find a renewed enthusiasm for spending time with his son, and both appeared to thrive.

When he was not in school, Dunnie McBakery worked with his father on the part of his family's farm that Jake had managed to keep. Jake and Betty were both working again and had managed to improve the family's finances enough to move out of the trailer and repair to a livable condition the old farmhouse that had belonged to Jake's grandparents. Father and son were seen together all the time around the community, and Dunnie was enthusiastic about learning what his father could teach him. If anything, Jake McBakery was too involved and even talked with his son about quitting school, when he got old enough, in order to do farm work full-time. Jake McBakery attended AA meetings, he was always prompt for appointments with the social workers, and he was nothing but "yes, ma'am" and "no, ma'am" when asked to do or not do something in relation to the child. The family had not been this happy since before Bennie McBakery was killed.

Sandra Miller also recognized that one side of Jake McBakery was equal parts dark and fragile. Her visits to the home usually took place around suppertime, when Jake had come in from the fields, Betty could be there, and Dunnie was working on homework, so most of the time they sat around the kitchen table. She came to realize that there were a few topics Jake McBakery would or could not discuss. On several occasions she asked him about the circumstances of hitting his son, and each time, his face flushed red and his shoulders hunched as if he had been assaulted. After a few minutes, he would lean back in his seat, cross his arms, and rock the chair backwards on two legs. He admitted to "having a temper."

The second time they tried to talk about it, Sandra Miller pursued the issue. "Yes, but do you know when it's about to get out of control? And can you recognize when you're about to lose it?"

He sputtered out, embarrassedly, "Well, Miss Miller, I guess me and just about anybody within ten miles knows when I'm mad," and there was obvious sarcasm in his tone. She responded more to the sarcasm than to the anger and the hurt, and she pressed him further. "Yes, but I want to know what you are going to do to keep it in check?"

He looked down at his feet and said simply, "Yes, ma'am."

She had not asked him a "yes, ma'am" kind of question and was ready to go further, but she looked at him directly and saw a look of anger and hurt and hate that frightened her. She had never seen someone's face glow red with rage while he struggled to pretend he was feeling something else.

Nevertheless, when the psychiatrists in the hospital got everyone together for the meeting to determine how to help Dunnie now, Sandra Miller had nothing but praise for the efforts of both Jake and Betty McBakery. After two weeks had gone by with the child on medication and receiving counseling, there was agreement all around that Dunnie was returning "to his old self." However, two days passed during which the hospital was unable to contact the parents, so Sandra Miller was asked to go to the house with word of a projected discharge date for Dunnie.

Sandra Miller was not entirely comfortable arriving at the McBakery house unannounced, but some worry and urgency called for this visit. She pulled into the driveway just as an early-season hurricane moving up from the Gulf of Mexico spawned a storm that drew thunder, lightning, and a heavy sheet of rain over the house and car. Although it was still hours before sunset, the clouds had brought to the farm an early darkness interrupted only by frequent bursts of lightening. She pulled her car up the driveway, plowing through a small river of draining water, and through an open window, she could see Jake McBakery sitting at the kitchen table.

Despite being able to pull her car up closely to the porch steps, she was well soaked by the wind-driven rain as she negotiated the opening and closing of the car door and use of the umbrella. She jerked open the screen door without knocking in order to escape the downpour as quickly as possible, doing her best to keep from splashing water inside the house.

It took her a full minute to take out a tissue from her purse and clean her glasses, and only then did she actually look at Jake McBakery. He had not moved from his seat to help her, and he sat stone-faced without speaking, glaring at her. His eyes were reddened, he had several days' growth of beard, and there was a look on his face she had not seen before. The open half-empty liquor bottle on the table spoke for itself. She was terrified and turned to leave, but at that very moment, a bolt of lightening struck a power pole, cutting out the lights. The room went completely dark, lit only by the storm's continuing flashes of light. Between the rolls of thunder, Sandra could hear the rain pounding the roof with such steady force that it sounded like a train passing by.

As her eyes became somewhat accustomed to the dim light, she watched Jake McBakery stagger to a cabinet and retrieve a flashlight. He shined it directly in her face and then sat down again at the table, balancing the light on its end so that the beam pointed upwards. The thin, faint ray of light stretched from tabletop to ceiling and lit the kitchen only enough to give the objects in the room an eerie glow and to throw shadows on Jake's face, making him look even more ominous and grotesque.

Sandra Miller was terrified but paralyzed by her fear. She sat down tentatively in the chair closest to her. She tried to think of something to say. "Is Betty home?"

"No...b'lieve she's gone for good this time."

The social worker didn't know whether Jake was aware of her fear. A minute passed in full silence, and then he spoke, "Thought you came to talk...so talk!"

She responded, "Mr. McBakery, I think I'll come back when you are feeling better..." and rose to leave.

"No! You came to talk...talk!" he screamed at her, then slapping the tabletop with both open palms. She sat back down and began to cry. He ignored her and took another drink.

She forced the tears to stop and began again, "The hospital..."

"The hospital? The goddamn hospital?" he roared in a drunken sing-song cadence, filled with sarcasm and rage, making fists with his hands. "Some of the same goddamned people that...first they told me that boy was retarded...and then last year...they...them...those...people...tells me he's not. And now he's in the goddamn crazy house, pumped full of drugs. And what now...you come to tell me he's OK again? Is that what you come to tell me? Is it...*is it*?" His voice rose to a crescendo of anger with the last two words. He threw the half-filled glass of liquor, and it crashed and shattered against the wall above her head, showering liquid and glass on her.

She bolted through the kitchen door, knocking over her chair and leaving her bag behind. Jake McBakery let out a loud laugh and followed behind her. Her foot slipped on the top step and she went down hard on her back into the mud at the bottom of the steps. Dazed but not seriously injured, she pulled herself up by the car door handle, somehow managing to hold on to her glasses. She pulled hard on the latch, but the door would not-open. She was standing face-to-face with Jake McBakery in the driving rain, his hand pressed against the window glass, keeping her from opening the door. He smiled an angry smirk of victory down at her as she slid back to the ground.

"You forgot your purse, Miss Miller," he said in a mock polite tone, lifting the bag to the level of her eyes. He dropped her bag into the mud beside her, turned, and walked away. She climbed into the car, covering the seat with mud and splashing water over the dashboard and on the inside of the windows. Wiping her face with only her hands and blouse, she started the car and sped down the driveway, but in her haste and fear, she swerved too far to the right and slid into a ditch. The car was stuck fast. The rear wheels spun and whined and dug a pair of deep holes into the soggy ground, but the car did not move.

Jake McBakery was dancing in the rain in the driveway, laughing loud and angry cackles of delight. He slapped his knees and fell over twice before he composed himself and approached the car. He yelled through the window, "Looks like you gotchurself a little trouble there, Miss Miller. Now why don't you just come on back inside while I get my truck and pull you out of there?"

They squinted at each other through the fogged window glass. She could not speak. He put his hand to his ear in a mock gesture of waiting for her to speak and then yelled, "Suit your goddamn self, bitch!" Sandra Miller sat crying and shaking as she watched Jake McBakery walk away from her through the rain and toward the house.

Jake McBakery had been drinking for less than an hour and was still on the way up from the effects of the alcohol. He felt that special chemical euphoria and power that nothing else in the world had come close to giving him—not God, not sex, not love—and the veil of shadows lifted from his eyes. He had spent the last two weeks with a tightness in the pit of his stomach that grew until it pressed against his lungs, closed up his throat, and burned the breath completely out of him. For two days, the waves of panic had rolled over him, the hair had stood up hot and sticky on the back of his neck, cold chills had come in spurts, and a veil of darkness had come down over his eyes, fading out the colors of the world and leaving him in a place and time of only black and white. There were only two choices: drink or die.

As he walked away from the car in which Sandra Miller cowered, he celebrated the fact that the knot in his stomach had dissolved in alcohol. He spread his arms out wide and filled his lungs with the cool wet air. The rain poured over him and washed the fire from his face and the sticky sweat from the back of his neck. He splashed and played in the rain like a child. He knew that this feeling would not last, that soon enough, the veil would come crashing down harder than before, but at the moment, he did not care. What he felt was some kind of blessing, a miracle, and he relished it completely. His skin tingled and stood up in cool gooseflesh in the soothing rain. He felt a surge of power and in his mind saw himself pulling her out of the car and showing her what he was capable of doing.

It took him about ten minutes to position his truck and attach the chain, bumper to bumper. It seemed like hours to Sandra Miller, who tried with little success to dry her eyes and stop her hands from shaking. She wondered if she could even drive the car if he was really going to let her go.

Before he pulled out the car, Jake went back into the house and brought out a clean dry towel. The rain had slowed but had not ended. He offered her the towel, but she shook her head no that she would not open the window.

"Look, lady…you're just goin' to run off the road again if you don't wipe off those windows," he shouted through the glass. She couldn't be sure it wasn't a trick, and the image of putting his hands on the top of the half-opened window and ripping it off did go through his mind. But when she did roll it down just enough to receive the dry towel, the two of them were face to face again. Her look of complete helplessness confirmed his supreme triumph over her. It was not necessary to assault her further. He danced a drunken jig back to his truck and pulled the chain taut. He growled in unison with the sound of his engine as he pulled her car free. He got out and unhitched the chains.

"Okay now…you're all set. You can go now…get on down the road now." He spoke to her in a mocking, patronizing way, as if he were an adult helping a small child. She eased the car onto the paved road and disappeared into the storm.

Jake McBakery stood watching the car and reflexively reached into his shirt pocket for a cigarette. Pulling out the pack, he saw it was soaked, and he crushed it with his hand. He filled with rage at himself for being so stupid to think he could smoke a cigarette in the driving rain. He ripped apart the cigarettes, threw them to the ground, and stamped on them with both feet. This was not enough. His anger grew. With his right fist he slammed the door of the truck, and then again and again and again until his hand was a distorted bleeding lump with bone sticking out from the back. He sat down in the mud and started to cry. But he felt no pain. He wiped the tears and rain from his eyes and thought about the hiding places in the barn where he had stored several bottles of liquor.

He pulled himself up from the ground and ran stumbling into the barn, kicking aside the loose hay to reveal the first of the bottles of whiskey and gin. He opened a bottle and drank straight from it, sinking down into the soft bed of straw and hay. His anger had lessened, but the feeling of power was fading too. He knew what was happening. He remembered the words of a song that talked about the ride on the way up. It said you still had to "meet yourself on the way back down." He cried and sang to himself. He didn't want to come back down and knew he had to keep drinking to keep going up. But still, he knew he would indeed soon be coming back down.

He made himself think about some of the good things that he always thought about when he was this drunk. He thought about his high school football days and the time that he did something really special. He called all of it back to his memory. He saw where all of the other football players were standing during that special game. He was an average football player on an unremarkable team. He knew this. But he still remembered that one night, that ball high in the air, just how it felt when it dropped into his hands and how the crowd screamed as he crossed the goal line.

Jake McBakery had scored a touchdown!

Not only did he score the first one of the night; he even scored again. It happened a second time that same night. It was glorious. Yes, that was the right word...glorious! No one at that game thought Jake McBakery would ever catch a touchdown pass, not even one, but then he ran down that field a second time, broke free from the players chasing him, saw the ball coming at him in a perfect spiral and felt it land so softly in his hands; he pulled it tight to his belly and ran to the left, then to the right, and again into the end zone. Yes. Glorious! He ran back to the bench with the crowd screaming and his teammates pounding him on the shoulders.

Wild! That's how they were—the crowd, the cheerleaders, the teammates. They knocked him to the ground with congratulations. He remembered it all. He called it back to memory as one entreats an old friend for company. The band played. The cheerleaders leapt and twirled. He saw them now in front of him. They were there, with him now. They did all of this for him...because of him.

He shifted his position in the straw and took another drink. He could see the clock on the football scoreboard running down. Time was running out. The game was almost over. He blinked his eyes and tried to stop it. This time he would stop it; he would keep the memory...no, not the memory, the game...he would keep the game alive and it would never end. He took another drink and hunched the muscles in his back and shoulders. He wanted to feel the strength of a man that could drag another man across the goal line. He flexed the muscles of his thighs and thought about the last few steps into the end zone.

This was the high point of Jake McBakery's football-playing, and it was enough to get him invited to the right parties, where he met Betty Houston, a sad mousy girl who, like Jake, stood off by herself. But he was holding hands with her before the night was over. She quit school, pregnant at seventeen, and they had a quick, small wedding, but some of that was the best that Jake McBakery ever had, even better than football. And now he was sure she was gone for the last time. Betty was gone. Bennie was gone. Dunnie was...well...the tears came again.

More drinks didn't work. He was no longer on the way up. He struggled to his feet, found a rope, and made a makeshift noose and slipped it around his neck. He tried to find a place to tie it and something to jump from, but he was too drunk. He tied it to the doorpost of a horse stall and then found a barrel to lean over, away from the stall. He figured if he leaned just right the barrel would roll over and it would cut the air and the blood so that he would first pass out, and then if he was lucky, he would lean there just long enough to die.

The call to Sandra Miller earlier that day, to see why no one had heard from Dunnie's parents in two days, came from the psychiatrist on Dunnie's ward. Lee called Mary McBakery with the same question. Mary had been to the hospital twice to meet with Lee, who wanted confirmation of some family information that she had heard from others. Lee talked openly to Mary McBakery about the case, which would have been viewed as a transgression of confidentiality in some people's eyes. Lee justified it by saying she needed to know the truth. And when Lee called Mary McBakery with the information that Jake had not been seen or heard from for two days, the older woman knew something was terribly wrong.

Mary McBakery arrived at the barn just as Jake McBakery was passing out from strangulation. She pushed him off and away from the barrel and loosened the noose on his neck, and he began breathing on his own. He did not regain consciousness until the next day in the hospital. The police arrived fifteen minutes after Mary McBakery, alerted by a frantic, mostly incoherent call from Sandra Miller from a roadside gas station. Mary McBakery rode with the drunken, muddied, bloodied man to the hospital in the police car, cradling his head in her lap, holding a makeshift bandage around his hand.

When they arrived at the emergency room, they were greeted by a doctor who showed obvious contempt for Jake McBakery's situation. He told them that he had more important things to do than take care of "hopeless drunks" and that they could just sit out in the waiting room until everyone else was seen. Mary McBakery stood directly in front of the doctor who was more than a head taller than she and told him that if Jake McBakery did not get prompt medical treatment, she would leave the hospital with the doctor's job and with certain key parts of the doctor's anatomy in her purse.

Cooler heads intervened and appropriate care was delivered. She accompanied the patient through the evaluation, the X-ray of his injuries, the bandaging of his hand, and his admission to the ward. No one even hinted that she was not welcome along the way. Throughout the course of events, Lee lurked unseen across the large open emergency department. When Jake McBakery left for the ward, Lee took Mary McBakery by the arm and suggested that she had done all she needed to do. The two women left together to find a quiet place to talk and review the events of the day.

They sat down in the office of the chaplain just across the hall from the emergency room and talked for an hour, a conversation that was not easy. Mary McBakery began by telling Lee that this was the last thing she was going to do for the McBakery family and by asking Lee to please not call her anymore. "Jake McBakery is not going to thank me for what I did today. I never liked him, and I don't think he likes me. If he thinks about me at all, I'm nothing but a meddling old fool...and the rest of the family can just go to hell as far as I care."

Lee saw that the older woman had dried mud and droppings of the man's blood on her hands and forearms and that mud and blood had splattered over her shoes and feet. She left the room briefly and came back with a pan of soapy water and a cloth. Without saying anything, she washed Mary McBakery's hands and arms and then removed her shoes and washed her feet. The entire process was completed in silence until Mary McBakery spoke. "You know, you won't be true to the Bible if you dry my feet with that towel, but I don't think you have enough of those blond curly locks to do it with your hair."

Lee knew enough about the Bible to understand the reference and both burst out laughing, and then Mary McBakery cried. Lee replied, "Now let's see here, who is supposed to be Jesus and...are you Mary Magdalene or is that me?"

"Thank you," said the older woman softly. She composed herself and smiled.

Lee then tried to comfort Mary by telling her that she had called Mary only partly because of Dunnie, that Lee had also wanted a reason to get back in touch. This did have a grain of truth, but in the business of trying to complete a medical residency in pediatrics, many things go on hold, so it was only a small grain. But this comment and the washing of her hands and feet touched Mary McBakery, and she suggested that they try to start over, to meet as something other than two people trying to rescue the McBakerys. Lee answered that she would like that very much and that she was entering the third year of her training experience, so there would be more time and she would make time.

"And I'll come to Chapel Hill," answered Mary McBakery. "I don't want to sit around at home...surrounded by all that old stuff. I'll come to you. Let's make a time."

# CHAPTER 12

# FINAL CHAPTER, OR NOT

## September 1981, at a sidewalk café in Chapel Hill

After that first afternoon with his cousin and Mary McBakery, John Randt was aware that something had developed between the two of them that did not include him. He told himself that this did not really matter, since the McBakery family was not his family, and since it was not something to which he gave a lot of thought. But when he accidentally stumbled back into that family in California, and it seemed inevitable that he would share what he found with Mary McBakery, he brought it up with Dr. Kingdon. His mentor encouraged him to do some psychological work on his connection to the older woman, because even though she was not really family, it would still give him a learning opportunity related to families. He recommended that John write to her.

John wrote letters to each of the women, suggesting that the three of them get together to hear some "fascinating genealogical information about the McBakery family" that he had discovered in California. In his letter to Mary McBakery, he tried to be cheerful and chatty, but he also included just a few lines about his work in the clinic, with comments about being face-to-face with real suffering and pain and musing about how some people seem to have more than their share of life's hardship. He was conscious of wanting to impress her, of wanting her to see that even though he'd only lived just under twenty-five years, he did have some degree of worldliness about him.

She wrote him back a short letter that was anything but chatty or cheerful, and she limited her response to a one-paragraph reply to his implied existential question:

*Dear John,*

*If you are asking me why bad things happen to good people, read the Bible. In it, you will find no promise of anything other than hardship in this life. I don't know if you believe that Adam and Eve and Lucifer were real, or like some people today, that the Bible is just a little bit of history and a lot of poetry. As for me, I don't know, but either way the message is the same: we live in a broken world and only in the next life is there a chance for anything more.*

Upon reading her reply, he felt rebuked and somewhat foolish, in addition to feeling ignored and excluded. He wondered whether he should even bother to pursue all this, but she did add in a postscript that she would be happy to meet with him at any time they could work it out, so he persevered.

In the two months following Jake McBakery's emergency room visit, the two women met five or six times for lunch or dinner but almost never spoke about the McBakery family. Lee got to know the older woman's life before and beyond her marriage to Louis McBakery and was pleased that she was becoming part of that life. Mary McBakery told Lee of taking first steps to free herself of the role of keeper of the flame for the family into which she married. She was giving away items from the "archive room" in the house in which she lived, and she was talking about moving, going to a retirement home of some sort.

Lee was surprised to find how little interested in family relationships Mary McBakery turned out to be. The older woman seemed to take no notice of the fact that Lee now referred to John as her cousin, although she was pretty sure she introduced him as her husband at the reunion. They talked about the McBakery family only enough to arrange with John a meeting time to hear his "big secret." John had asked that the older woman bring the collection of papers from which Mary McBakery once read them the account of the lost twin boys. They finally agreed to meet for lunch at a sidewalk café on Franklin Street in Chapel Hill. They met on a crisp fall afternoon that boasted a stunning blue and cloudless sky. The women had spent the morning shopping and were dressed in new clothes, both sporting red hats. When John spotted them from down the street, they were giggling and talking, and he thought they looked like a pair of silly teenagers.

After John sat down and lunch was ordered, the two women made him wait to tell his story until they had told theirs. Even though he didn't want to just blurt out that he had solved the family mystery, he was eager to tell the story, but as the

Jake story unfolded, he became more interested and let them tell it in the manner that they had chosen. They told all the details, and with Lee involved at the hospital, and Mary McBakery knowing what she knew from her vantage, there was considerable detail to be told. The story came out in a fashion every bit at as dark as it had happened, and the pain of the events at the McBakery farm, especially the events in the barn and in the hospital, was not lost on John.

Mary McBakery took great care to make sure John understood that this series of events had been the "final chapter of her taking care of the McBakery mess." She explained this with the understanding that John Randt was in the process of looking for understanding of his own family, and she took pains to say words that defined her state of mind as different from his. She said she wanted to be sensitive, but "I'm not you," she pointed out.

She was speaking directly to him when she said, "I don't want in any way to make light of what you are doing with your own family, but there's also the thing that sometimes...the thing a person has to do...is put some distance in the picture...between people...I hope you can see what I'm saying."

John did feel disappointed. He was still thinking of Mary McBakery as the family historian, and even with his brief estrangement from his parents, he had never experienced the kind of injury from family that would lead him to seek an enduring distance. He understood that his need was different and that others simply would not share his enthusiasm for this kind of thing. He wondered whether he really should tell them what he had discovered. Maybe it was something he should just keep to himself. Maybe there were others in that family that would want to know it.

John ultimately responded to Mary McBakery with a reply that delayed the question of whether to tell them about his discovery of the fate of the twin boys: "I understand what you're saying, and I hear that you're through with...with...being in charge of all that...stuff with the trouble in the family...but can I tell you a funny story...not really about them...kind of about them...but mainly about where I worked this summer?"

Mary McBakery felt relief that John seemed to be changing the subject and that as far as she could tell, he did not appear to be injured or angry that she was not willing to talk about her past anymore. At that point, the waiter came and delivered their order. The comfort of good food combined with this new direction of the dinner conversation lightened the atmosphere of the gathering, and John proceeded with his contribution in an upbeat manner. He took his time in setting the stage for his storytelling. He described the clinic in the old Victorian house just north of San Francisco and introduced the characters with whom he had worked and from whom he had learned over the last four months.

He explained that one of his educational tasks was to present a case to all the different people in the clinic, from the analyst to the feminist to the gray-robed guru who was trying to redefine his own identity. The case he chose was a somewhat creatively elaborated presentation of the McBakery family. He admitted to making up a few things to juice up the case for his own educational purposes and said he figured no one would ever know the difference with the full distance of a country between the clinic and the McBakerys. When he said this, he winked at Lee, who smiled as if she got the message that she was the one who taught him how to tell a lie.

"So the first guy I approached happened to be Rondahl, the one who wore robes and looked like Jesus. When I started giving him the history, it didn't look like he was paying any attention to me; it looked like he was filling out some forms or something, so I just stopped, and it took him more than a minute to notice I wasn't talking any more." John laughed at this point while relating the story, but added that it didn't seem funny at the moment it happened. He continued the account, saying that Rondahl at that point held up a glossy brochure and said two words, "Municipal Bonds."

John admitted to having been quite irritated that he had spent real energy to prepare his presentation, and this man who was supposed to be his teacher was fully preoccupied with other matters. When Rondahl turned back to his financial forms and proceeded to work on them, ignoring John's presence in the room, John blurted out a question that was intended to be sarcastic.

"But what about karma…or cosmic consciousness?"

Rondahl was clearly startled and turned back to him with a reply that seemed to come from the heart: "But they're *tax free*!" John left the room without further interaction, and the two never spoke again. He did see him a few weeks later in the parking lot, holding the purse and other belongings of a clearly pregnant woman who was throwing up, likely with morning sickness. He recognized the woman as a teller at the bank where had his account. This seemed to explain a little about the focus on municipal bonds.

Lee laughed so hard that she almost choked on a bite of food. Mary McBakery appreciated the frustrating nature of the interaction that John described, but lacking the context that the younger people brought to the event, she was mostly puzzled. Lee took a moment to point the older woman's attention to a variety of storefront displays nearby and posters on lamp posts that made reference to "new age" concepts, people dressed in robes and promising wisdom and enlightenment. Mary McBakery replied that it looked interesting and that she just might look into what that was all about.

"Wait, it gets better," John added. Next he sought the guidance of Dr. Holland-Hill as to how to address the family issues. She listened to his overview and then asked him how certain things made him feel. When he began his answer, she interrupted him and pointed out that she had asked him what he "felt," not what he "thought."

She gave him a short lecture about the difference between thoughts and feelings. "A feeling is like sadness, or anger, or a sense of longing. You described an opinion...quite different from a feeling," she explained. John tried to explain that certainly there were aspects of the McBakery troubles that mad him sad and angry, but since he wasn't really a part of that family, he wasn't much affected by the feelings that one might experience.

Dr. Holland-Hill became animated and emotional. "But doesn't it offend your sense of personhood to know that there are people that suffer at the hands of others...weak helpless people who have no way to defend themselves?"

"Yes..." John replied tentatively, sensing that she was going somewhere with this line of questioning but not sure exactly where, "I guess that's why I want to do this kind of work."

"But if you're going to do this kind of work, you must sort out your feelings, get in touch with what angers you, what you would give your life for, what you would give up anything for...what would that be? When you figure out what you feel about things, it becomes easy to decide what to do to help people." Dr. Holland-Hill was becoming tearful, and John wished that despite the value of feelings, he could return to the intellectual world. He started to say that he didn't really think he would give his life for any of the families he was seeing at the clinic, but he feared this would not be well-received.

After a few long moments of silence, Dr. Holland-Hill composed herself and asked him to continue the presentation. At this point, he described the encounter between Lee and Dunnie McBakery in the trailer park. She interrupted him again: "Are you saying that this all takes place in the rural South?" He gave her some more information about demographics and geography, confirming her perception.

"I don't have anything to help you with," she stated bluntly. "You are talking about a culture that cannot use psychotherapy. It's a failed, illegitimate way of life, and the best that child can do is get out, get out any way he can. I know. I spent some time in that world, but I got out. You know what the difference is between the bumper sticker on a therapist's car and a bumper sticker on a redneck's car?"

It took John a moment to realize that she was telling him a joke. The swing of emotions and the change of topics, from a case presentation to "redneck" jokes, had John completely off balance.

Dr. Holland-Hill gave the punch line: "The therapist's bumper sticker says, 'Think Globally, Act Locally'; the redneck's says, 'You Can Have My Gun When You Tear It from My Cold Dead Fingers.'" And she let out a laugh and started talking about how Southerners pronounce certain words as she imitated a Deep South accent. John didn't walk from the room. He ran.

Mary McBakery, Lee, and John laughed so loudly that others at the café looked at them disapprovingly. "And I didn't stop running until I was all the way through the garden and down to the water," John concluded.

"Wait, wait," Lee put in as she stopped her laughter with a few deep breaths. "What was that story you told me about the shrink that was going to pull the woman's ears off...please don't tell me you went to see him."

"Actually, I did, and you know, he was the most reasonable of all of them.

Mostly, he was just a good listener," said John.

"He sounded like a man of action to me—grab the ears and pull..." continued Lee, trying to keep the humor going.

"No, really, let me tell you about him. Truly, he was the most helpful of all of them," John replied, adding what he said was the most helpful piece of advice he got from anyone in the clinic: "When you don't know what to do, just shut up and listen. It all starts with the ability to really listen."

John went on to describe a few more things about his time with the psychoanalyst, who disclosed that he too had spent a lot of time "knocking on some doors," trying to learn about his family history. He told John that he had actually received some criticism from other analysts who thought he needed to be more "traditional," meaning stay in the office.

"He sounds more like you than that other pack of rats," offered Lee.

John went on for so long about his conversations with Dr. Raymond Sorrow that the finer points of the interaction with the psychoanalyst were mostly lost on Lee and Mary McBakery, so the story trailed off, simply stopping rather than concluding. The older woman broke the short silence with, "But all of that is not what you came all the way from California to tell us, is it? What do you have in that little blue folder there?"

She was referring to a thin folder of papers that John had picked up and put back down several times during the meal, not finding the right time to show the photographs of the drawings by Adam McBakery that he had returned to get from the Carson Mansion.

John decided that he indeed did not want to leave there without showing what he had found. He opened the folder and placed the copies of the four Adam McBakery pencil caricatures on the table in front of them. Mary McBakery gave out a little gasp and picked up the historical papers that John had asked her to bring. She flipped through the papers and found a section that took a full minute for her to read before she turned back to the others. Although the picture of the peddler and boys in the wagon was the one that John thought would be most informative, she was focused on another. She read Winnie Callum McBakery's summary of Sarah McBakery's diary, in which the boys' mother, the matriarch of this family, had described her memories of her lost sons. This included her memory about the boys running after the frightened horse pulling the plow, with the father laughing and the mother issuing warnings. Here was a picture of that memory, on paper, right in front of them, drawn by a man in California that could be no one other than one of the lost boys.

John Randt had accepted that Mary McBakery might dismiss the photos of the drawings as unimportant, but he could tell now that her reaction was something else entirely. What he did not know, what Mary McBakery had not talked about in a long time, was that there was a period of time in her life that she, even more than Winnie Callum, was obsessed with finding out what had happened to these children. Having been an orphan herself, it had become vital to her that someone care what happens to lost children. She had pursued the story of the boys with such a degree of obsession that she became a nuisance to others in the family. Her husband ultimately scolded her for this and told her that she needed to get on with her own life and leave the dead alone.

John and Lee sat patiently watching her as she tried to absorb this new information. She looked silently at the pictures and then turned more pages of the historical record. As the certainty of the facts and the truth of this discovery set in, Mary McBakery experienced something similar to what people have reported experiencing when they believed they were facing death. Key moments of her life danced in her head. Without her consciously calling for them, memories raced though her mind. She saw dim and distorted pictures of her parents who had died when she was so young; she replayed in her mind her arrival at the orphanage; she remembered hearing sermons given by the sometimes mad minister that had introduced her to the Bible; she saw the face of the child molester that everyone had called Grandpa; and she remembered the time she stood guard halfway between the orphanage and the field-day celebration while the two other girls carried out their collective plan to put fire to all the buildings save one, thus ending that chapter in her life.

These memories and more came rushing back to Mary McBakery: her marriage to Louis McBakery, the birth of her two sons, and incident upon incident of her trying but not quite managing to fit in and be a part of that new family. All these thoughts and memories came so quickly into her mind that it was as if she had experienced them all simultaneously. These pictures in front of her represented her most distant connection to the past—the lost twin boys—and now, sitting with her now were two young people who in the last few months had invested as much of their energy and their emotion in her as had anyone since Louis McBakery had died. Running through all of this, from the most distant time to the most present, was a single chord of life, encompassing everything and everyone, and she was a part of it, part of a world where lost boys were found and orphans were claimed. She felt an outpouring of love for her dead husband. She was a part of this, tied to it all by the thread of history. She put her face in her hands and wept.

John and Lee were caught up in the emotion and cried with her, although they were far from understanding what had just happened. Mary could not speak of it—not just yet—and she soon dried her eyes and regained her composure. She looked at John and said simply, "How did you do it?"

John told them the entire story—from the minute he saw the sign in the antique store, to the delightful and aggravating Buster Griffin and their trip to the big house, and all the way to the moment he stood in front of the drawings by Adam McBakery and was convinced it was the story he came to find. Then he corrected himself: he was actually looking for the Randts, not the McBakerys, but in the four months he was there, he turned over every rock in the state and could find no sign that there was ever a Randt in California. When he said this, Lee kicked him under the table and gave him a stern look that at first he did not understand. Then he realized that Mary McBakery still did not know. She had no idea that she was not related to the other two people present.

By that time, they had been sitting in the café for more than two hours, the check had arrived, and people were waiting in line to be seated. John took Lee's cue—her kick, that is—to move along to the business of paying, tipping, and leaving. Outside the restaurant, as they walked down the street, the older woman leaned over and wrapped her arm around Lee's waist. She made an excuse of feeling a little dizzy, but in reality she just wanted some kind of physical contact and comfort. Lee felt a little uneasy and suggested that John might be a better person to hang onto, but Mary McBakery joked that he might think she was "making a pass" at him, and she smiled at him.

None of the three, for their own reasons, was quite ready to say good-bye to the others, so they found a small park just off the street and sat down on benches to talk for a few more minutes. John accepted more praise and admiration for having solved the mystery, and ultimately the conversation turned to what was next for each of them. John spoke first to say that he had a job offer with Dr. Kingdon, his hero and mentor. It wasn't the job he thought he would have, but Dr. Kingdon had procured a grant to build computerized files of genealogical information to help families more easily find out about their backgrounds. John said he didn't really know much about computers, and he really couldn't understand the value of putting the information on computers. "I mean, what's the advantage?" he mused. "You still have to print it out and loan it to the other libraries, don't you? You still have to get to the library." But he added that Dr. Kingdon had been right about a lot of other things, so he was just going to trust him on this one, too. It was a pretty good first job.

"Do you think you will ever see the old man in California again…what was his name?" asked Lee.

"Buster Griffin," John laughed. "I'm sure I will. I just wrote him a letter telling him I was going to go to China and that I was on the trail of Joseph McBakery, but I needed money and wondered if he would go along and pay our way. I can just see him cursing and stomping and fussing about money."

Lee spoke next. "Well, I guess I've decided that I can't be a fraud any longer."

Damn, thought John, saying in his mind, I've got a lump on my shin from where she kicked me and now she's going to tell her the whole story about how we crashed the reunion.

John was wrong. Lee continued, "You know how I talk sometimes about wanting to be a surgeon? Well, I've done it. I got accepted for an internship in general surgery."

"Wait a minute," interrupted the older woman, "You've been through what, two years, two and a half, in this one kind of doctor training…and now you start all over?"

"That's pretty much it," Lee replied. "UNC has programs all over North Carolina in community hospitals, and they have open slots from time to time that you don't have to go through the formal matching thing to get, and I applied and they said come on, so…it's not Johns Hopkins, but it's a real internship and who knows where it will go."

Then it was Mary McBakery's turn. "What about you?" John asked. "I mean, with you cutting all your ties to the McBakery family, what does the future hold for you?"

"Well, I guess it would be a good idea for me to get in touch with Winnie Callum…uh…whatever her last name is now…the one that wrote up this history. I told you that they ran her out of the state, didn't I? I don't know if she cares, but I'll give her a chance to tell me that she doesn't care…that we found out about those twin boys, if I can get a copy of those pictures to send to her."

Mary McBakery looked down at the ground and told them about one more thing. Jake McBakery had been calling her for over a week now, saying he wanted to come over and thank her for what she did. He told her over the phone that he and Betty were getting along again, and Dunnie was doing better, and it was thanks to her that he was still alive.

"You know, we never liked each other, but I guess I should visit with him one time. You know what? I'll make him help me clean out all that junk that I won't need now that I'm getting out of there." She added that somebody in the family needed to take care of it. But it wasn't because she cared a flip about any of them, and she sure wouldn't be putting up with any of their mess anymore.

John said goodbye to the two women, and they walked away to their cars. He stayed behind, watching people go by. It was the week after Labor Day.The students had come back to town, and their parents had gone, leaving their children to their own adventures.

He took out a journal and wrote some notes to himself, a habit he had developed when trying to understand something. He had no idea what went on inside Mary McBakery when he presented her with the drawings of the lost boys. And he was curious about the relationship that was developing between the two women, feeling happy for them and feeling somewhat left out at the same time. But he was sure that he wanted to spend the rest of his life trying to figure out these kinds of things, maybe even getting paid for doing it. He thought that nothing could possibly be better than earning a living by snooping around in other people's lives. He was eager to begin working with Dr. Kingdon and to talk to him about all of this.

He wrote, "Two women. An older one who keeps talking about not taking care of people anymore but can't stop doing it. A young woman who talks about being burdened by taking care of everybody but decides that she can do it as long as she does it with a knife in her hands. That's scary.

And me, I need to write another letter to Buster Griffin, tell him about the woman I'm dating and that I'm not going to get so busy that I forget to get married and have children.

Life is good. The possibilities are enormous.

Sept. 11, 1981"

# Epilogue: A Reconstruction

The History of the McBakery Family 1850–1950
By
Winnie Callum and Mary Wallace McBakery
(Except from part four of nine: originally published in June 1987)
*Reprinted by permission of* The Southern Genealogical Prospector, *"The premier southern magazine of genealogical discovery"*

Sarah McBakery was almost certainly at the funeral of her sister Ella, who died in childbirth in 1874. After the loss of her twin boys and her husband, Sarah had traveled from Colorado to be with her sister. Since there is little information about the actual events surrounding Ella's death, except for several family diaries kept intermittently in the years that followed, one can only speculate about Sarah's state of mind at that time.

What we know from Sarah's own diaries is that she was ambivalent about the offer from Ella's widower, John, to stay there and help raise the child that had survived Ella's death. She must have wondered when the deaths and losses would end, and the best information available is that she drove a hard bargain with John McBakery before agreeing to invest in living again. He had recently left the employ of a store and had signed on to be an apprentice in a bank, and he needed to be there at the bank every day. Sarah used this as leverage, it seems, as she recorded in her diary one month after Ella's death.

She wrote, "I will not beg. I will not work for a pauper's wage. If I am to again provide for the care of others, I will be paid and paid well."

John and Sarah married a year after Ella died, and whatever agreement Sarah struck with him to result in their moving to Asheville and leaving Ella and John's child behind is not known to any living person; nor is it known how the child came to be raised with a last name that was not McBakery. It is perhaps enough to say that the daughter left behind lived a life of integrity, married, and had children and grandchildren, some of whom came to North Carolina in the middle of the twentieth century and took the body of John Phillip McBakery back to Virginia, where he lies today beside his first wife, Ella.

One entry in Sarah McBakery's diary deserves particular mention. She wrote this section in a hand that was more deliberate than her everyday offerings and notated that she was writing it to clarify an incident reported in an Asheville newspaper. In the summer of 1876, a man came to her door "for the purpose of extorting money" from her and John McBakery. The man claimed to be Will McBakery, her first husband, and when he was not granted entry to the house, he became violent. Sarah called the police, who arrested the man, according to the newspaper account, but no court record of what transpired regarding the arrest exsists. Sarah McBakery went into considerable detail in her diary explaining why this man could not have been her first husband. No record of a Will or William McBakery is otherwise found in any court record or legal document of any kind in North Carolina or Virginia that dates to a time after Sarah's return from Colorado.

Full text available from
*The Genealogical Prospector*
Concord, N.C.

978-0-595-36955-
0-595-36955-3

Printed in the United States
94552LV00004B/517-564/A

9 780595 369553